peter quinones

Postmodern Deconstruction Madhouse

iUniverse

POSTMODERN DECONSTRUCTION MADHOUSE

iUniverse books may be ordered through booksellers or by contacting:

iUniverse
1663 Liberty Drive
Bloomington, IN 47403
www.iuniverse.com
1-800-Authors (1-800-288-4677)

ISBN: 978-1-4917-9183-7 (sc)
ISBN: 978-1-4917-9184-4 (e)

Print information available on the last page.

iUniverse rev. date: 11/18/2016

Table of Contents

The Fizz Notorio

Shortly after earning her bachelor's in business administration on a campus where the most popular majors seemed to be headphones, cell phones, and Instagram, Eve Patricia accepted the offer of an interview for an entry level job with a negotiations firm. As part of the process she was asked to take a test in which she was presented with twenty fictitious negotiating scenarios – some involved business deals, some concerned international geopolitical crises, some focused on family tensions and personal relationships. In each case her task was to identify what she believed to be the most prudent course of action – trying to work out a compromise, sticking to her guns without giving in an inch, or complete capitulation and retreat.

Later, after gaining the position, her new employers told her that she had correctly chosen in seventeen of the twenty. They didn't say which three she fumbled but in the three month training and probationary period she often reflected on the matter and felt certain that the ones she must have flubbed disproportionately included considerations of proxemics.

Proxemics – a field to which she had never given too much thought or attention in her twenty four years, but her bosses and colleagues – seasoned professional negotiators all – put such an emphasis on it that she was quite able, in a short time, to appreciate its usefulness way beyond the confines of work, out in the galaxy of everyday life.

This appreciation broke into glorious blossom when Eve Patricia began her dalliance with Harshwine, a gentleman twice her age.

Now - men of limited force and power in the Johnson have to assess, from their own individual vantage point, how this will impact upon a relationship with any given woman – not with women in general, in archetype or Platonic Form, but very specifically with this woman here or that one over there. Harshwine of necessity had made himself a master of the process by his middle forties. He'd learned that he could pack a wallop with a cornucopia of women through showmanship and spectacle – he didn't need Viagra or Cialis.

The first tool in Harshwine's arsenal of seduction was his apartment on an upper floor of a spanking new high rise in Long Island City, Queens, with spectacular views of the east side of Manhattan, the East River, the 59th Street Bridge, and the Triboro and Hell's Gate Bridges. The place was a firebomb of visual razzle dazzle, and at night the contribution of the city lights was romantic beyond speech.

Eve Patricia was an example of a woman whose initial doubts and resistance could be nibbled away at by this sensational apartment. At twenty four she had a good job, was quite intelligent, loaded with sharp wit, was emotionally stable and mature, good looking and in shape – a catch and a half. And so the question naturally would arise: what would such an obviously desirable young woman be doing fucking around with an older man who could barely slide the sausage in one out of every five tries – not to mention that when he did it wasn't very fulfilling at all?

Thusly it is that the puzzles of the human heart are pondered.

At the prime of the getting to know each other phase, sitting in a Greek café on 30th Avenue, they spoke to each other about religious belief. She was a Christian by birth, indifferent and certainly non practicing, but she had yet to experience anything like the kind of nihilism on the cosmic level as expressed by Harshwine. "We're tiny insects crawling on an insignificant revolving rock, thrown in a remote corner of an infinite universe – but we can't live like that. We can't live our lives that way. That's our problem. We have to infuse everything we are, have, and do with meaning. That's it. The proverbial human condition – we have to live as if our lives have meaning." He spoke with feeling; never before had she known a guy who could emote so urgently and yet, simultaneously, communicate the savory in the mixture of seared tuna burger, fries, and coleslaw that was pulsating through his mouth, on his tongue, in the spaces between his teeth. And he did it without spitting food.

They bantered back and forth about the art gallery where they first met and the art that was exhibited therein. For Eve Patricia it was a tributary of her job – the firm was negotiating some issues on behalf of the gallery, which was being sued by several artists it had represented in the past. Harshwine – she surmised, because it wasn't entirely clear – had some kind of friendship with the gallery owner and several of the artists the owner was currently representing. Once or twice he gave hints of having been a player in the art world of Manhattan in the eighties.

Initially she had conducted a deep internal struggle about spending the night with him in his Long Island City place with the drop dead views.

"I want you to stay," he'd said. "But I don't grovel. I'm not going to ask you more than once." He had sharp features – his face was like a metal spike. There was something edgily contumacious about the way it combined with his "don't grovel" personality that turned her on a bit.

Groggily opening her eyes to her first morning in the place the word *proxemics* clamored through her mind like a twister. The first principle of this discipline was that people felt most comfortable, totally relaxed, in three environments – their home, their place of work, and their cars. Eve Patricia felt comfortable in Harshwine's bed, which she took to be a good sign even if it contradicted the law.

Was it a kind of Feng-Shui thing that he had what appeared to be hundreds of fortunes from Chinese fortune cookies everywhere in his apartment? They were even in the bed, mixed up among the sheets; she'd slept soundly on them all night.

> TO AVOID CRITICISM DO NOTHING,
> SAY NOTHING, BE NOTHING.
>
> BY LISTENING, YOU WILL LEARN TRUTHS.
> BY HEARING, YOU WILL ONLY LEARN
> HALF TRUTHS.
>
> THE GREATEST GENEROSITY IS NON-
> ATTACHMENT.
>
> WHAT ABOUT THE BABIES? WHAT ABOUT
> THE SUNSHINE?

His pad was best defined as a gigantic studio. The first thing Eve Patricia always did when waking to the day was clean the sleep crust out of the corners of her eyes with the tip of a index finger, and as she did so here her line of sight focused on Harshwine across the room rather silently doing Hindu squats. Before her senses could perceive much else the land line phone rang sharply twice and an ancient answering machine picked up. "Hi this is Harshwine, please leave a message."

"Harshwine baby! It's Prockahoon. Got your message. Ten o'clock is fine. My father's check arrived here yesterday. Look forward to meeting you and your new young chickie wickie! Later bro!" Click.

Eve Patricia laughed, calling "Prockahoon?" across the room. "What's his first name?"

Harshwine grunted with effort, his body moving up and down. "Good morning to you too. I don't even know…Lester? Les. Richard? Dick. All I've ever called him for so long is Prock or Prockahoon that I don't even remember his first name."

Eve Patricia busted out in laughter every time she heard someone named Richard called Dick; in grade school she had had a classmate named Richard Holder – thus, unfortunately, Dick Holder. The memory always floated in whenever she heard the names.

A fugacious instant carried a stab, a twinge, a pang of buyer's remorse through the valves of her heart – he was so much older! Yet it quickly passed.

"You got some weirdo friends, old man," she called out, rolling gleefully around in the sea of Chinese fortunes.

"Don't knock Prockahoon. He's a great person to have in your Rolodex. He's a networking machine. He has forty eight hundred friends on Facebook."

"What? Forty eight hundred?"

"No lie."

He was picking up the pace with the Hindu squats, getting into a consequential groove. His body created a silhouette against a section of bare wall while his actual physical body moved against the gray, bitter, incoming winter light. "Animals in the wild," he had stated to her the previous evening while they cuddled, "are, universally and without exception, in better shape than human beings. And they don't lift weights or work out with machines. So what explains it?" She'd given a slight shake of her to indicate she had no idea and then her attention drifted while he continued talking. She was a bit zoned out – his world, his concepts, his ideas, the whole way he lived, everything was so alien. Just before they had hopped into bed and he launched into his speech about animals he had been in the bathroom taking a shower and she stood in the main living quarters studying his collection of compact discs that was stored in tall shelves against one of the walls, shelves that resembled bookcases. They went to the ceiling; he had several stools on hand so as to be able to access the upper shelves.

CDs were objects that she was only peripherally aware of as existents, in the way a Baby Boomer might be aware of a black and white television with no remote, six channels, and rabbit ears. Fascinated, she studied the rows of them, running her index finger along the spines. The principal source of her curiosity consisted in this: out of the hundreds and hundreds of discs that there were she realized she had never heard of any of the artists – not one. Was it possible? He'd been kissing her aggressively just moments before, while a kind of music played that startled her with the crashing urgency of its metaphysical sweep – she had reached across his body to seize the disc on the night table beside the bed – Tony Williams, *Civilization.*

Back to morning: she asks, "So is this the exercise you said you do five hundred of every morning?"

"You're such a wise ass, little girl. I said I do three hundred, five days a week, working my way up to five hundred."

"You got any coffee?"

"Right there on the counter. I only have standard ground 'n' pound supermarket coffee, no Raspberry Melon Asteroid Latte."

The phone rang again before she was able to get out of the bed and she recognized Prockahoon's voice a second time, this time singing lyrics to the tune of *The Surrey with The Fringe On Top:*

"Ducks and geese will all come a honkin'

When we go out tonight honky tonkin'
We will ride them beautiful horses
Though we should be takin' some night school courses"

5

Click.

Eve Patricia was wildly amused. "What! What the hell was that? Those aren't the right words! He made those words up!"

"You know that song, huh?"

"Of course I know it! I played Ado Annie in my high school production of *Oklahoma!*"

"That's one of Prockahoon's hobbies, he ad libs lyrics to Rodgers and Hammerstein songs." He smiled – a consuetudinary fleer of resignation and of circumstances. "He's, um, he's just a little offbeat."

"Just a hunch – you've been friends a long time?"

"A long, long time. Look – he's a weirdo. When we visit him you'll see exactly what I mean. Just ride the flow."

"The first time he called he said he had his father's check – what's that all about?"

Harshwine hesitated, his lips shut tight and twisted up in a sign of internal debate. "His father sends him money from Florida every month. He uses it to pay me the rent."

"Does he work?"

"He's some kind of statistician but obviously it doesn't pay much. He can't hold a real job. His credit is destroyed."

"Go on. What's wrong, trouble breathing? Should an old man like you be talking and working out at the same time?"

"You know, for such a fine young hoochie mama you certainly are a wiseass."

"Just playing with you!"

"I know." They both smiled.

"How many so far?"

"Sixty."

"On the way to three hundred? Should I just come back tomorrow?"

"Make the coffee."

"What's next, Zen? Are you going to sit cross legged on the floor and contemplate an empty flower pot for sixteen hours?" Giggling, she rose from the bed. The evening before, three times, he had noticed that the way she got out of bed was extraordinary – instead of just rolling out of it on the side she shimmied her way down to the foot of the bed and got up from there.

"Everything's right on the counter in the kitchenette. Now if you can shut your wisenheimer, sarcastic ass twenty four year old mouth I really need to bear down and concentrate so we can get out of here and start the day." The plan for the day was to walk the length of Crescent Street to Broadway then along Broadway to Steinway, visiting Prockahoon and several other of Harhswine's tenants. He owned nothing but, rather, rented apartments and then sublet them to others for virtually full price, the profit being in the fact that he sublet one apartment to two, sometimes three roommates who all paid full price. It was an astonishing arrangement that he had learned from Paul Zane Pilzer. The apartments were all over Long Island City and Astoria. And yet, to fill his days and nights with meaning, he himself worked as a common waiter in the kind of sprawling, gargantuan diner owned by Greeks which used to be everywhere in New York but were rapidly succumbing to modernity.

"Great," said Eve Patricia. She stretched her foxy arms and legs mightily, opened her mouth to give a craterlike yawn of morn, and got to making the coffee. The kitchenette's huge window looked right down at the Queensboro Plaza elevated subway station. The evening before, as they embarked from the 7 train, she couldn't believe the throngs of people on the platform and the stairs but now the station seemed almost abandoned in this early hour.

Prockahoon called a third time. "Did I tell you I was tutoring some ESL students? Fairly advanced. Much more drive and motivation than native born American kids. One assignment was to write about something they saw on the news. Kid picks some union on strike out west someplace. She writes "The rank and file union members were menstruating on a picket line outside the corporate offices." Broke my heart to have to correct her in front of the whole class that she meant demonstrating."

Completely nude and, to her own surprise, completely uninhibited she made the coffee while feeling the crinkle of two Chinese fortunes under each bare foot:

OUR PURPOSE IN LIFE IS NOT TO GET AHEAD
OF OTHER PEOPLE – BUT TO GET AHEAD OF
OURSELVES.

TURBULENCE IS A LIFE FORCE, IT IS
OPPORTUNITY.
LET'S LOVE TURBULENCE AND USE IT FOR
CHANGE.

IF YOU HAVE NO CRITICS YOU'LL LIKELY HAVE
NO SUCCESS.

WHAT ABOUT THE BABIES? WHAT ABOUT THE
SUNSHINE?

In spite of, almost in defiance of, the ferine weather she felt not at all chilly. The steam in the apartment blasted through the pipes with the sensory vigor of a stalking leopard.

The truth was that something about the whole scene was exciting her in new and novel ways. Here she was – a fairly typical, average girl from the Midwest trying to make a life for herself in New York, a story that has been repeated hundreds of thousands of times down through the ages. And here she was with this sexy (if mostly impotent) older guy with the insane apartment and "don't grovel" attitude; somehow he communicated to her by everything he did that he was thrilled to be with a sexy young babe but that he really wouldn't be any big deal if she were to go. This was something so different from the way guys her own age behaved with her – like meek little lapdogs – that it spun her mind. And, in spite of his lack of, err, situation he had sexually intoxicated her the previous afternoon and evening in ways guys her own age had never even approached before.

In Queens Center he had dropped two hundred bucks on a pair of Steve Madden sneakers she said she liked without even blinking, like he was buying her a hot dog. And here she was thinking they were just having fun window shopping! The wad of bills he yanked out of his jeans pocket made her cover her mouth with her hand in surprise. She was able to intuit that something about him was way, way off – his level of cultural sophistication didn't square with being a server in a diner. At the art gallery he had moved fluidly among the high and mighty folk with grace and ease, speaking the language fluently: light and shadow, line and form, Meyer Schapiro and Clement Greenberg. He held a glass of wine in his hand with practiced elegance, but his first spoken words to Eve Patricia were coarse and tasteless (he had been formally introduced to her about twenty minutes earlier, merely nodding politely). "You see this cunt Miranda Freewell in the crimson gown? Have you ever met such a pretender in your life? The way her lipstick matches the carnation on her boyfriend's tux?"

She stood naked with her arms folded across her chest watching his old electric coffee maker huff and puff and drip drip drip. She was enjoying luxuriating in a new feeling, a bold female confidence, a completely new vista of experience. Everything felt right.

She poured out two cups of coffee and sipped her own. She said "About last night."

"Yeah?" He was sweating now, locked into a steady rhythm.

"Are we going to do that again?"

"You're damn right we are. Ha! You like that?"

"Loved it."

"Great."

"No one's ever spoken to me like that before."

"I'm sure."

"You're grunting. With the effort."

"Of course I'm grunting with the effort. You think this is easy?"

Here she made the decision to have a little fun with her older man. She replicated the exact pitch, cadence, and syllable count of his remarks. "Bah (Of) bah (course) bah (I'm) bah-bah (grunting) bah (with) bah (the) bah-bah (effort)." And she began to mimic his execution of the exercise the revered Hindu squat, playing up awkwardness and goofiness out of all rational proportion. Both laughed – she out of genuine delight and he placatingly. It was an advantage of experience he enjoyed merely because he was older – he could plausibly fake a placating laugh and present it as a soldier of reality.

He said, "Is this what you do as a dispute resolution professional? Practice mockery?" That made her laugh even harder.

While he was off dressing and getting ready, out of a deep curiosity about the ancient answering machine with the little miniature cassette tape that recorded messages, she hit the "Play Messages" button and was rewarded not with messages but most of an entire conversation. The voice of a damaged female said, "Many people have had children. Some even became golf players. This I know from reason."

Harshwine was heard to answer "You can't say 'golf players'. 'Golfers' would be the proper term."

"Maybe 'golfers' is more common, but surely golf players is proper English?"

"No, it isn't. You wouldn't say 'swim players', would you? No, you'd say 'swimmers'." And the message cut off with a sharp beep.

Another slice of a conversation played on the next, this time with a different woman who said, "Between the implants and the partial dentures I would say go for the implants."

He replied, "I think I agree with you. I think the dentures feel too heavy in your mouth."

After a time both were sufficiently coffeed up to dress and embark. Again he noticed an unusual habit of hers – she put on both sock and shoe on one foot first, leaving one bare and one completely ready before doing sock and shoe on the other. While she was bent over in the chair he observed therewithal that she was a willing and enthusiastic participant in the mostly completed overall societal tack to a wholly commoditized concupiscence; in other words, she liked to wear Victoria's Secret thongs.

Crescent Street was cold and windy. The day was gray. They moved arm in arm past some rundown apartment buildings.

"Talk some erotic shit to me," she said suddenly out of the blue. "Whisper in my ear."

"You're such a bad girl."

"Come on. Turn me on old man."

"Here?"

"Yes. Here. Now."

He pulled her hat back over her ear. They came to a halt at a red light and he whispered into her ear the following: "That postmodernism is indefinable is a truism. However, it can be described as a set of critical, strategic and rhetorical practices employing concepts such as difference, repetition, the trace, the simulacrum, and hyperreality to destabilize other concepts such as presence, identity, historical progress, epistemic certainty, and the univocity of meaning."

She threw her head back and her face looked like St. Theresa in Bernini's statue. "Oh you sexy motherfucker," she breathed.

They came upon a greasy spoon. A feeble middle aged woman was fighting the wind, trying to open the door to get in but the wind kept blowing it shut. She tried once, twice, three times before she finally almost had it open but a strong gust came in and blew it shut once more with a slam. The final insult came when the wind blew her hat off her head and whisked it off to eternity. The woman howled and ran off down the street.

At what was still not the nicest part of Crescent Street they came upon an unusually large, beautiful and well kept home with a white picket fence around it and an impeccably manicured lawn. What? Here? It was if a fleet of giant helicopters had picked it off a movie set and lifted it to Crescent Street. There was a terse handwritten message on the front gate, held there with industrial tape:

DEAR DOGS: Please curb your human pets.

They stopped for the briefest instant to read the note, then continued without remark. Eve Patricia intuited a pair of connate eyes observing them through curtains.

"I'm so curious now about this guy Prockahoon. Tell me some more about him."

"Umm..I think possibly he's a little too intent on creating magnificent experiences that bring beauty to the soul."

"What do you mean?"

"He has a lot of unmastered sorrow."

In the middle of the animated conversation about the oddities of Prockahoon that followed - which they were about to experience any moment now - they finally reached the intersection of Crescent Street and Broadway, where the following epic vision greeted them.

Six or seven homeless men, evidently acting in concert, crouched low with their trousers and underwear down around their ankles, shitting into the palms of their hands and flinging the clumps of shit at people. For a second the surreal character of the scene froze Harshwine and Eve Patricia in their tracks but in the ensuing few seconds a humble, frail elderly lady dressed in her Sunday best took a furious log right in the back of the head; the force of the blow might have been from a brick as it knocked her forward a couple of steps. She staggered, clutching at a parking meter for support. People were screaming, guiding young children to safety, waving their arms, diving for cover. Shards of feces slapped into a fruit stand, a car windshield, a bicycle that was chained to a pole. The shit seemed to stream out of the bodies of the homeless men in unending supply. Their shriveled cocks and balls stood in the raw, chilly air like petrified prunes. One of the men had some kind of pukey green liquid ground into, frozen into, the scum white of his beard. Several of them bounced on their toes like athletes, fecal balls in hand, stalking for possible targets. Eve Patricia thought she saw a young girl with shit dripping off her eyebrows, hanging like icicles, but she couldn't be sure of this. In a moment police cars with blaring sirens screeched up. Officers advanced upon the men brandishing riot shields for protection against any errant projectiles.

Like many in the area, Eve Patricia had been snapping pics and shooting video with her cell phone all the while. She was usually not one for such activity but this was extraordinary and she felt it was her duty to mankind to have some record of this occurrence. No one would ever believe it. It was the kind of episode that in previous epochs lived only in the cracks of sidewalks and the cracks of history.

The building where Prockahoon lived could justifiably be called a tenement. Seeing this gave Eve Patricia a look into Harshwine's character that she previously hadn't had. She reminded herself that he was renting this apartment from the landlord, say, for a thousand dollars a month and then subletting it to Prockahoon and someone else who each, in turn, paid a thousand dollars a month to Harshwine. Eve Patricia had once taken a history class on the classic robber barons – Commodore Vanderbilt, Jay Gould, Amasa Stone. It fascinated her.

In the hallway of the building they took off their hats and gloves, still partially in shock, and waited to be buzzed in. Their cheeks were red and their thoughts askew.

"Did that just really happen?"

"Yup. We just witnessed a small army of homeless men throwing shit around," she said dazedly, as if giving a report to an uninvolved third party.

The buzzer buzzed with sharp anger, a crow in flight. Harshwine turned the knob and nudged the door open with his shoulder. There was no elevator in the building; they went into the vestibule of broken dreams and up the creaking staircase to the fifth floor. Sounds mogated outward from behind apartment doors: a woman moaning in pain, children screaming, mindless cartoon laughter, conversation in indecipherable foreign languages, pounding music. A child's tricycle with a flat tire was outside one door, upside down and precarious. Eve Patricia thought she saw a discarded, half chewed pork chop on a step but she couldn't be certain.

When at last they arrived at the apartment Eve Patricia smiled upon noticing Chinese fortunes taped to the door, under the peephole in a vertical line:

EVEN A HARE BITES WHEN CORNERED.

GOVERN A FAMILY AS YOU WOULD COOK A SMALL FISH – VERY GENTLY.

TO KNOW THE ROAD AHEAD, ASK THOSE COMING BACK.

THE PALEST INK IS BETTER THAN THE MOST RETENTIVE MEMORY.

WHAT ABOUT THE BABIES? WHAT ABOUT THE ECOSYSTEM?

"The bell doesn't work." Harshwine made a fist, ready to pound on the door, but she grabbed him by the wrist to stop the knock. "What?" he asked, surprised and a trifle irked.

She pointed with her index finger at the peephole. A bloodshot eyeball had silently appeared behind the glass. The eyelid fluttered up and down a couple of times.

"Prockie babes, wassup!" Harshwine smiled.

The eye completely disappeared.

"Prockahoon!" Harshwine called.

Nothing. Harshwine rapped on the door and called some more.

Nothing, again. Eve Patricia knocked on the door with both fists playfully, emulating the movements of a rock and roll drummer. Only quiet in return.

"Shit, I have to pee like crazy. Prock, come on! It's Evie and I!!" But nothing happened. After several more moments of pleading and imploring they gave up and turned to go, flabbergasted. Then the door opened.

There stood a gentleman about Harshwine's age whose bushy eyebrows met, forming a V. His cheeks had crazy, even insane hollows but his nose retained stateliness and augustness whereas his eyes had the aforementioned bloodshot zing of rock stars after they thoroughly trash ten thousand dollar a night hotel suites. Unattended hair grew out of his ears. The black hair on top of his head was mangled and his facial skin bore craters, the remains of thousands of pimples. A very loose blue T shirt, old soiled jeans, and snakeskin boots – once probably awesome but now most deplorable and ungratifying – covered most of the pasty undernourished body. All the fingernails were bitten and chewed except for the pinky of the left hand, which had been allowed to grow long, thick, and disgusting.

As Harshwine simply stood there saying nothing, Eve Patricia extended a hand and said, "Mr. Prockahoon, at last we meet! I've heard a lot about you. My name is Eve Patricia."

"This isn't Prockahoon," Harshwine said.

Rumor People

Virginia was sapiosexual, which accounted for entries in her diary such as the following:

"Obituary after obituary after obituary after obituary discussed the neoteric news of the passing of Evan S. Connell and somehow neglected mentioning *The Diary of a Rapist* and his amazing books of historical essays and book length poems – how? Why?

If you were the stereotypical visitor from Mars, the proverbial blank slate, the person who is fine with the observation that the Wikipedia article on Lindsay Lohan is longer than the one on Mozart, you'd leave these death notices with the belief that Connell's principal contributions to our literature were a history book about Custer and a pair of companion novels sublet by Merchant-Ivory."

Even in repose, in moments of soft reflection, Virginia's face was a composite of knee weakening natural beauty and profound lines and crevices that were the biological manifestation of acute biographical mistakes and stress. She ran two miles every morning, worked with weights three times a week, was never without pepper spray in her bag, always had fresh flowers in her apartment whether supplied by herself or a paramour (she loved the smell) and allowed herself a big, juicy, sloppy cheeseburger every Sunday afternoon at Sinners N Saints. Ritualistically, after her Sunday meal, she popped in a few doors down at The Mane Event for some beauty business. She was forty six years old. Notable features of her past included a moderate inheritance from her family which, coupled with her own wise financial ways, permitted her to be semi retired; and an older brother who had committed suicide by drinking a quart of Drano. He had existed before the era of headphones, cell phones, and Instagram.

At one point her unrelenting quest to meet intellectuals who could chill her spine in bed led her to volunteer her time a few nights a week at one of Manhattan's oldest chess clubs. It's little known to the public as a whole but serious, high level chess players are some of the weirdest motherfuckers on Earth. There is a great American tradition of this: Bobby Fischer, Paul Morphy, Harry Nelson Pillsbury. At Virginia's club there was one guy who talked to the chess pieces. Another clearly massaged himself underneath the table. A third had the wildest hair in all of human endeavor – it looked like he poured a bucket of water over himself and then stuck his finger in the nearest socket. A fourth wore the same tomato sauce stained white dress shirt every day for weeks on end.

Virginia saw that she had to do some recalculating. She'd anticipated being around dignified, urbane men and instead of this the whole place was a freak show.

Then along came Rolando Carspidrain, shortly after she'd already given the club authorities notice that she would be out of there in a few more days.

"It's amazing," he told her on their first coffee date. "My father and his friends used to wait eight weeks to get a copy of the latest chess magazines from Russia. Now, with the internet, it's instantaneous – you can follow the games as they're being played, in real time."

Cougar mode was something new to Virginia; he was twenty eight.

"Obviously making a living at chess is something that isn't possible in America, as it is in Europe and Asia. It's a hand to mouth existence." The piano player Bill Evans once remarked that he never paid attention to any song lyrics - that to him the singer's voice was just another instrument. This was exactly how Virginia felt, listening to Rolando – his voice was music. His words were sounds, beautiful sounds. And he always smelled so good!

But it occurred to her that he was waiting for her to say something, so she asked him how he was making his living, what he was doing to supplement his chess studies.

"I work in a lab overnight, from midnight till eight AM," he declared.

"What kind of lab?"

He lowered his eyes to examine his folded hands on the table, the first time his steady, quietly provocative gaze had left her face. "I'm a nocturnal penile tumescence monitor."

"Do you know what attracted me to you, Rolando?"

"My good looks and gorgeous body?"

"Those came after."

"Oh. Then what?"

"The book you sit there reading between your games, or while your opponent is thinking about his next move."

"Ah! So you're attracted to the book, not to me."

"No, to you." She laughed. "I'm attracted to you because of the fact that you're reading the book. I like a man with brains."

The first brief date having gone well, they set up a second, this time for dinner at Sinners N Saints. There were any number of old burnouts in the regular crowd there who lusted after Virginia, one or two with decades long ardor, and of course she knew this. There was no harm, so she felt, in playfully cracking a couple of hearts open.

Sinners N Saints was a neighborhood haunt tucked away in the forgotten world of Henry James in the ground floor of a red brick townhouse on Barrow Street deep in the West Village. It boasted a grizzled clientele consisting of faltering scholars, has-been-before-they-ever-were painters and sculptors, bohemian leftovers from the Beat Generation wall to wall, and exceptionally high Zagat ratings for décor which the ones for food and service didn't quite match. Had smoking inside restaurants still been legal the room would have been enveloped in a constant cloud. In the main it was a dark compartment permeated with shots of golden light throughout and postmodern, minimalist wrought iron tables and chairs. The aroma of beef was everywhere.

Each table, as well as a seemingly uncountable number of small shelves on all the walls, had two twelve inch high statues atop them – one sinner and one saint. The saints were all done in realistic, lifelike color while the sinners were white Italian statues of pulverized stone and marble from the Vittoria Collection.

The only kind of music that ever came through the speakers – ever – was red hot bebop.

Virginia showed up dressed to kill. Rolando was already there, humble and discreet and dignified as always except for the one long lock of his jet black hair that perpetually slashed across his face. In the course of their coffee meeting he'd brushed it away from his eyes dozens of times, driving Virginia wild. She had a name for it that she entertained privately, to herself – his shocky lock.

The hostess seemingly came with the place, was part of the building. Virginia could not remember coming there even a single time and not seeing her around.

"Two," Rolando told her authoritatively and unnecessarily.

"Duh," she shot back. She looked past his shoulder at Virginia. "Hey there Gin Gin!"

"Wassup! How are you baby?"

"I'm fine. I didn't know you were a cradle robber Ginny."

Of course, Virginia was caparisoned for this reaction. Carspidrain was not. There were a pack of gruff male wags at the bar, spearheaded by the great unrequited admirer of Virginia's named Kentuckus Plowfinger, and they all studied the entrance of the couple with instantaneous hankering heartburn; with ambrosial shock; and with premonitions of onanism for themselves.

The hostess led them to a table near the back, turning sideways to squeeze between the chairs as she did so, and Virginia and Rolando followed suit. She made him go first and as they went she held his arm and whispered in his ear, "This place makes the best cheeseburgers in New York!"

"You definitely never struck me as a cheeseburger chick, Virginia."

"I'm really not but once a week I think you can allow yourself to be bad."

Once seated Virginia could feel the stabbing glare of hate like the rays of the sun on her back. Kentuckus Plowfinger was scowling at the bar. She made a dramatic performance of taking her Motrin, dragging out the process of taking the bottle out of her purse and shaking two pills out of it. She let the pills dissolve on her tongue rather than swallowing them.

The wait staff functioned like the bromidic well oiled machine; most were college kids from NYU but some were older folks who, much like the hostess, had been employed there since the dawn of creation.

Mexican busboys quickly and efficiently brought a basket of rolls and glasses of water, and a female server appeared seconds thereafter, adjusting professorial tortoise shell glasses on the bridge of her nose. These were riotously incongruent with her spiked auburn buzz cut. She spoke.

"Good evening guys. Your saint tonight –"she nodded towards the two statues on the table – "is Saint Benedict. Benedict was born in Italy in the year 480 AD. He lived in a cave for three years praying to God. Sometimes a raven brought him food." Another, swifter, more utilitarian female server stuck her head into the mix, putting a hand on the shoulder of the first to indicate pause. She pointed at Rolando.

"A drink sir?"

"I'll take a Heineken, thanks."

"Heineken. And you Miss Ginny?"

"Everybody knows you here." Rolando laughed, amazed.

She grinned and touched him lightly on the wrist. "Mojito." The server nodded and split like a bolt.

The first continued, "Your sinner tonight is Pauline Viardot. She was the most successful seductress known to history. Legend has it that men committed suicide over her. Men who are thought to have done so include –"

Kentuckus Plowfinger inserted his drunken ass self just about here.

Of him this much was known: he was a discredited bootblack, banned from Pennsylvania Station. Beyond this piece of knowledge there was little available information about his past. And his biography seemed impenetrable – except to Virginia, who knew some things about him.

The swarthy good looks of Rolando – he quite resembled Mickey Rourke in *Diner* – had a desperately negative effect on Plowfinger.

As Plowfinger began to inject himself into Carspidrain's consciousness Carspidrain happened to be eavesdropping on a conversation at a nearby table. He was paying scant attention to Virginia, to Plowfinger, to the speechifyng server. A woman was asking her tablemates philosophically, "What, exactly, are toes? How would you define them? What are they?"

"I know," someone volunteered. "They're like these little sticks that come off the ends of your feet."

"Well, not by the hair of my Ginny Gin Gin," ejaculated Plowfinger with crabbedness. A vague air of the unwashed was about his body.

"Kenny," Virginia said with a deliberately false and exaggerated joy. "How nice it is to see you! Meet Rolando."

Due to an overall lack of facility in the most useful skill of the adjustment of the emotions, love often causes this: disaster.

Plowfinger ignored Rolando's outstretched hand and smile. Carspidrain, though young, had a fair degree of fluency in the human heart and could smell the malignity.

The rejection went back eight or so years; Plowfinger lived his life like Boldwood in *Far From The Madding Crowd*, a situation familiar to Virginia who had much acquaintance with the canon. It might well be that he had stuff from Vicky's Secret as well as jewelry all carefully packed in paper and inscribed in a fine fancy font -"Mrs. Bathsheba Boldwood" … err, "Mrs. Virginia Plowfinger."

Plowfinger was a silver ponytail with fingernails about a month beyond the clipping limit that most of us would categorize as comfortable, and a black and red checked lumberjack shirt.

Rolando heard someone nearby say to their tablemates "My parents say they know they must be close to the end because they get fewer and fewer Christmas cards every year. Their circle of friends is slowly dying off."

The first imbroglio connecting Virginia and Kentuckus happened quite some years before. Even then they knew each other casually, - by sight, not by name – from Sinners N Saints. Virginia was leasing herself a new car, and Plowfinger happened to be the finance manager in the dealership. This job entails doing the aftersale: selling Lojack, alarms, accessories, picking up money on the interest rates.

He had been struggling for months with inadequate production. Evidently his sales skills were in freefalling deterioration. He'd been given a warning – he had one month to pick it up or he was gone.

Not having any luck whatsoever with the things he was currently offering to his customers, he went out and found something new called Shatterproofing. He felt that this miracle product could be his salvation and was glad that, when he begged his bosses to let him try it, that they rolled their eyes but said OK.

As life would have it, this simple product would be the catalyst to kick off a groundswell of soaring atomic jealousy.

Plowfinger knew nothing of the science behind the product, just that the essence of it was that once it was applied to a glass surface it would render it shatterproof. The sales rep from Shatterproofing brought in an easel, a large pane of glass, and a hammer.

"Hit it," he told Plowfinger with an abundance of enthusiasm. "Go ahead, whack it with the hammer."

"You can't be serious."

"I'm totally serious. Go ahead, hit it!"

So Plowfinger sighed and struck it a mighty blow once, twice, three times – nothing. Impressive!

Virginia, of course, was the very first customer he got a chance to try out this glorious new product with.

"Your saint tonight," a waiter at a nearby table was saying, continuing valiantly in spite of the horrible scene Plowfinger was making just inches behind him, "is Saint Martin de Porres. He loved all the creatures of God, even the lowly mice who did so much damage to the linens in the friary."

Another female server at a different table was also trying gamely to behave normally even as Plowfinger behaved beyond the bounds of all decency to Virginia and Rolando: "Your sinner tonight is Mata Hari…"

Sitting in Plowfinger's office that night in the past Virginia listened carefully to his offers. She politely declined everything. While he droned on unconvincingly about Lojack she looked through the window and saw an ancient Chinese woman pushing a shopping cart filled to the brim with empty cans and bottles, a ubiquitous New York scene. They scavenged for them everywhere, collected them, and brought them to the supermarkets to claim the refundable deposit. You needed to collect twenty cans to make a dollar, and it was hard to believe but these women were buying houses, cash, with the money they redeemed from soda cans.

"I don't think I need Lojack Kenny," she observed. "But what's this?" She nodded to the pane of glass resting on the easel.

"Glad you asked! This is our newest product. It's called Shatterproofing. It protects your windows and windshield from shattering."

"Really? Now that's something I might be interested in. I've had some bad luck with my windshield, twice. Rocks on the BQE."

"Really now. So you know what a pain it is to have to replace a windshield. This will render all the glass on your car unbreakable, and you can residualize the cost of it in your lease."

"Yeah, but how do I know it will work?" she asked skeptically.

Plowfinger was ready with the hammer.

"You can't be serious," Virginia laughed.

"I'm totally serious. Here. Go ahead. Hit it, give the pane of glass a whack with this hammer! You won't believe your eyes!"

Quite obviously no one needs to be a clairvoyant to guess that when she wound up like a baseball pitcher and hit the glass with the weapon it exploded into hundreds of pieces. A detailed description of the incredible chaos that ensued is not necessary, is best left to the imagination; suffice to say that both of the principals bled, and badly. A spiniferous segment of the flying glass found its way into Plowfinger's forehead, causing him to prate like a piglet while rolling on the floor.

Virginia watched in horror as Plowfinger suddenly grabbed Rolando by the collar. Gasps, then a hush, fell over the room.

Being that it was only their second time out together Virginia, of course, couldn't possibly know everything there was to know about Rolando. She didn't know his favorite color, didn't know what sign he was, and didn't know he was a black belt in karate. Plowfinger completely misinterpreted Carspidrain's understated control of his anger and desire to defend himself as meekness, perhaps even cowardice, perhaps even fear.

Since the episode with the shattered glass Virginia and Kentuckus had remained friendly, and he asked her out many times – he seemed unable to understand that once a woman puts a man into the friend bag it is well nigh impossible for him to get himself out of it He was a pathetic wuss. He got fired from the car dealership and went into business for himself shining shoes in Penn Station until he was banned for life from that worthy locale. He grew bitter, resentful and spiteful towards Virginia.

One night - this was many years after the incident with the glass and about a year before Plowfinger caused the scene with Rolando at the restaurant - Virginia was a little unsteady on her feet, walking down her street, coming home at about two AM from a date with an engineer who had told her he was taking lessons on how to improve his "thrusting depth" as if this was a credential for something. Too, he had accused his cleaning lady of trying to piece together ribbons of paper he had shredded in his shredder, apparently with the intention of perpetrating identity theft. "This is the world we live in, you have to shred the shredded paper." Virginia was already tuned out, having decided to get drunk on his dime and never see him again.

Making her way down the street, she grew aware of a shopping cart full of all manner of cans and bottles parked in front of a house, and she could see and hear a furtive figure rummaging through the garbage cans and recycling cans in front of each and every residence on the block. An elderly Chinese woman, doubtless.

But no. It was Kentuckus Plowfinger. When he recognized Virginia staring at him, agog, with her mouth agape, he tried to cover his face with his arm so as not to be recognized.

In the seconds before he made the snap decision to take care of Plowfinger Rolando's eyes circled the main dining room of Sinners N Saints, taking in the view. A young man in his twenties was holding his burger to his mouth, jaws open to receive it, his eyes fixed on Rolando. A woman in her sixties stirred her drink on the table in front of her, eyes gazing down into it as though it were a crystal ball. A couple made out hungrily, ignoring their friends at the table with them who averted their eyes in embarrassment. The doors of the kitchen swung open and shut, servers and busboys going in and out of them at breakneck pace. A man in his forties drummed his hands on the table top in front of him, trying to keep time with some insane improvisation that came over the speakers.

Few who saw the kick would ever forget it; it probably became a viral sensation. In the first place, you could hardly believe a human being could get their leg so far back, behind, and over their own head. The force of the blow was so profound when Rolando's foot hit under Plowfinger's chin that it almost lifted Plowfinger off his feet. After the paramedics collected him the place, wobbly, took but a short time to return to normal.

"Virginia," Plowfinger begged that night when she saw him collecting cans and bottles. "Please. I beg of you. Can you keep this between us? Can you? This is the most embarrassing thing that's ever happened to me in my life. Please."

He didn't return to Sinners N Saints ever again after Rolando damn near kicked his head off his shoulders, but the happy couple did on a regular basis. Rolando was tickled pink by the mechanical statue of St. Blaise in the men's room, which was almost something out of an old time amusement park. This saint was the patron of people suffering from illnesses of the throat. The statue was a life size replica of Blaise (poorly painted indeed – the face was goofy). The statue was preposterous, in such poor taste that nobody could mistake it for anything but a joke. It looked like a contraption from a long lost carnival. When you stepped on a mat in front of it the arms and hands extended out toward you to bless your throat, and the robot mechanically croaked "Blessed be God!" Rolando immersed himself in this ritual ten times every time he visited the bathroom – he loved the feeling of St. Blaise's metal hands against his throat - and he wondered if there was a similar gag in the ladies room but he never remembered to ask Virginia.

She told him, as she had to, the saga of herself and Plowfinger, how she had happened, by complete random chance, to see him in two tremendously embarrassing situations and how she had rejected his many advances and pleadings throughout the years.

"Maybe you shouldn't have flaunted me in his face that way," Rolando speculated.

"Fuck him," Virginia replied.

One fine morning some months down the road as they were walking up Virginia's block on the way to her car he noticed a sign in the back window of a parked school bus. It said "THIS BUS HAS BEEN CHECKED FOR SLEEPING CHILDREN!" This struck Rolando as being an extraordinarily odd announcement, and he asked Virginia about it out of curiosity.

Virginia looked sensational in ripped jeans, a solid color tank top that was loose off one shoulder, and ankle length lace up boots in a tiger print pattern. Ever the vision of Woman In All Her Glory, she turned her face to the sun and explained that about a year or so before there had been much outrage and controversy when a school bus matron had failed to notice that a sleeping child was still in the back of a school bus that was subsequently parked in a lot and locked up for the night. The child spent the night horrified inside the bus while, outside of it, packs of wild attack dogs that roamed and protected the lot in the overnight barked and scratched and clawed at the bus windows for fourteen hours. The city council immediately sprung into action and passed a law about signs.

In the car Virginia said, "You've never told me much about your family Rolando. Why?"

"Oh…there's not so much to tell. You know."

"I don't know. Tell me something about it."

"Um… it's hard to know where to begin."

"You mentioned your father once. I guess he was a chess player?"

"Yeah. Actually there is a story I could tell you about my father. His life was pretty dull but his death was actually kind of exciting." Rolando was dressed completely in black, his dress shirt opened four buttons down. He brushed his shocky lock away from his eyes. He then said, somewhat astonishingly, "Obviously you can't make a living at chess in America. The neutralization of dust mites was a passion of his as well."

"What? His death was exciting? How?"

Her car was stopped at a red light behind a school bus. In the back of the bus, looking thorough the window down at Virginia and Rolando in the car, a group of boys began making obscene gestures at the two. One made jerking motions with his fist near his crotch; a second puffed up his cheeks and pumped his fist at his lips. Several gave the finger. One, predictably, dropped his trousers and pressed his bare ass cheeks against the glass. They all erupted in laughter at the obvious disgust of the couple in the car, at their own insatiable desire to say fuck off to any and all adults, and because their gestures and motions were, when you got down to it, actually sort of funny.

"This is school bus day I guess," Rolando said, leaning back in his seat and sighing. Prisms of sunlight were blinding him through the windshield. The light changed. The school bus turned off, and there was clear sailing ahead. Virginia zoomed the car up the street towards Eleventh Avenue. She asked him "What's this about your father's death being exciting?"

He turned to her with a sad expression that she had not seen on him previously; a kind of sadness that came forth from the bottom of the well, from the final reserve tank, from the last chance desperation emergency playbook. "In two thousand and six the funeral home where we waked my dad was shut down by the FBI."

"Why?"

"They were trafficking in black market body parts."

"What!"

"Yes. You could Google it if you want to read more. They were selling body parts on the black market." He told her the name of the funeral home.

"So what happened with…with your father?"

"Well, the FBI agents told us that dad's body might not be in his casket and they asked us if we wanted to do an exhumation."

"And?"

"We did it. They dug his casket up out of the ground and opened it."

"And?"

Once more they were at a red light. There was heavy traffic all around them, and to the right the mostly unseen skyscrapers of midtown Manhattan seemed to lie in wait to hear what Rolando had to say as well. She turned her attention off the road for a second to look at him; there were tears on his cheeks.

Often, towards the end of the beginning stages of a relationship, a person may have an epiphany in which it is revealed that the beloved is not, after all, a glorious cherub beamed down from the heavens but is, instead, merely a person who burps and pisses and farts just like everybody else. This is what happened here.

Virginia pulled her car off the avenue and into one of the mysterious side streets full of garages that dominate that part of town. Rolando watched her as she Googled the funeral home on her phone and read a couple of articles about the shocking scandal. She put her hand to her open mouth, then touched him gently on the wrist. "My God," she murmured. "Is it true?"

"It is," he said. "When they dug up my father's coffin and opened it his body wasn't there. It was a mannequin, a store dummy, and the casket was weighed down with bricks."

"Jesus Christ!"

"And that isn't the end of it either."

"They never found his body?"

"His body was cut up for body parts, Virginia."

"Oh my God."

"One day I got a call from a woman saying she needed to see me. The desperation in her voice was so overwhelming that I let her talk me into a meeting."

"Who was she?"

"She was an average woman in her forties who had had two discs in her neck removed and replaced with ones that were supposedly from a young organ donor."

"No- don't tell me."

"But she said that a couple of months after her operation her surgeon told her that it was likely these discs had come not from a legitimate, good hearted donor but rather from a lawbreaking funeral home and the discs most probably came from an older person who had no wish to be a donor. She had heard somehow that my father's corpse was one of those missing. She-" Rolando was crying openly now, weeping. He couldn't continue. He sat there sobbing and Virginia felt like shit, seeing now that her pressing him about his family had opened up this wound. They sat there silently with the car running.

Virginia rubbed his thigh with her hand. He composed himself somewhat. She backed the car up, straightened it out, and they were on crowded Eleventh Avenue again, heading uptown. She let the car swim in the traffic, its interior an uneasy cabin of thick emotional humidity, groping for a way to move the conversation, the relationship, forward.

"So how's your new job?" was what she came up with after a few minutes.

Rolando had left his night job in favor of a new opportunity at a travel agency. The office was finely adorned here and there with six foot high Greek and Roman columns upon which rested brochures of the capitals of Europe. This was curious since the only vacations anyone ever booked through the agency were trips to Florida or the Caribbean.

Carspidrain ignored the question and said, "Hey, let's hit The Highline. It's a nice day, we can do some great people watching and just walk around and do nothing important. How about it?"

Virginia appreciated, for the umpteenth time, his controlled sense of understatement. He was the living embodiment of the old adage that still waters run deep. "All right." She turned the car up 23rd street; they parked in a garage and, back on the pavement, gave a good performance as true sophisticated Manhattanites holding hands. A light breeze teased of summer as they ascended the stairs up to the main ramp of The Highline and they walked slowly, aimlessly, hand in hand, arms swinging, among the crowds.

Something had been lost between them, and Virginia felt bad about it. It hit at her in pangs. She had pushed the issue of his father too far, at the wrong time, in the wrong way, in true Men Are From Mars, Women Are From Venus style. As they walked she nuzzled his shoulder; he half patted, half stroked the hair on the top of her head. "Tell me again about the book you always sit reading at the chessboard."

"Again? Virginia."

"I never get tired of hearing it."

"I know."

"It's what first drew me to you."

"I know. I'd rather tell you how I love to rub my face in your hair. Your hair always smells so good."

They came upon a small crowd of people who were grouped in a circle around a rough looking man in jeans and a t shirt who was arguing ferociously with three middle aged Japanese business men in suits and ties. The man's t shirt said ROYAL FLUSH CORPORATION – *Your Dependable Source For All Your Portable Toilet Needs.* They ignored the brouhaha and kept walking. Illegally, in violation of the rules of The Highline, a kid whipped by on a skateboard.

Rolando said, "The reality of each individual is just as real to them as your own is to you. Think of all the collected facts of your own individual biography, from as far back as you can remember to this very moment, right here, right now. Everyone you ever meet in your life has such a history as well." He swept his arm to indicate the people all around them. "But we don't think of other people that way very often. In fact, we tend to think of most other people in our lives as scenery. Think of that parking lot attendant, that kid, we just interacted with for sixty seconds and will probably never see again in our entire lives. For all the impact he made on us he might as well have been a coat rack or a lawn mower. And yet he's a human being with a whole years long history of hopes and dreams and wishes and desires and likes and dislikes and loves and hates and good times and bad times that are just as real to him as ours are to us, but we'll never know anything about them — what they are and aren't, nothing. It's staggering."

They sat on a bench at a point at which the guard rails at the end of The Highline were literally inches from an ancient apartment building. Signs on the ground warned everyone to PROTECT THE PLANTS – STAY ON THE PATH. At this section the plant life was reddish orange brush.

"I could really, really love you if not for our ages," Virginia tactlessly blurted from left field. She instantly regretted it but his reaction was equally stoic and reserved.

"Me too," he almost whispered, succumbing quietly to fate and to reasonableness.

Her head was on his shoulder, a resigned physical expression of bittersweetness.

They sat looking out at the wild graffiti on the sides of buildings, at the fire escapes that snaked up out of the atmosphere, at the human circus of dignity and loss going by in both directions before their eyes. On a bench across from them sat a young mother and her child, maybe four years old, playing with a vivid pink Slinky.

Watching the child made Virginia think of her own children, long gone.

"Lunch?"

"Sure, I'm hungry."

"Let's stop at an ATM and go to French Fry Nation," an establishment that only took cash.

"Great baby, let's do it."

In the aftermath of the incident to follow next it became clear, it came to light, that Joan Jones had been warned several times about her dog, a 125 lb. brown Bullmastiff; that several neighbors of hers had complained to the authorities about it and its threatening, intimidating demeanor; that there had been an episode in which the dog had savagely bitten a child, although Joan Jones made the argument (successfully) that it was the child who had provoked the dog; and so forth. In other words this dog had a history.

The dog was muscular and powerful, and Joan Jones walked it proudly. She herself wasn't much —the dog was her foremost companion on Earth.

Someone had once given her a basket wire muzzle for the dog which she had immediately consigned to the garbage. In any case, Joan Jones and her 125 lb. Bullmastiff happened to be in the same enclosed bank of ATMs in Chelsea at the very same instant that Virginia and Rolando were there that afternoon. The dog was clearly agitated about something. As Rolando and Virginia entered the building a frightened looking pair of girls were exiting, one saying "People shouldn't be allowed to bring those big dogs into public places like this."

The dog jumped a little as Rolando stuck his card in the machine. Joan Jones absentmindedly pulled on the leash, paying more attention to her banking. Virginia displayed too much fear, too much nervousness. The dog could smell it on her, and this in turn fired up the already fired up animal. It came for her in a second, yanking free of Joan Jones' oblivious grip and ripping at Virginia with force and drama. As is the genetic code for this kind of dog, it didn't bark much but made low growling sounds, all the while sinking its fangs into Virginia's arm. The latter screamed in pain and in premonitions of immediate death. The dog got its teeth into her and swung its head violently from side to side.

"The mace!" Rolando screamed. "The mace! The mace in your bag! Mace the dog! Mace it!" But she couldn't, being paralyzed by both fear and agony. Rolando sprang into action – while Joan Jones wailed and people outside pressed their faces against the glass, looking on – and grabbed Virginia's bag off her free shoulder – the one the dog wasn't clamped onto – and found the mace.

When the pepper spray hit its eyes the dog went absolutely batshit crazy, howling in distress and harrowment such as no living thing should ever be made to suffer and flailing all its legs crazily, whimpering. Joan Jones went to the dog while it cowered in the corner; Rolando and Virginia staggered outside. An ambulance was already pulling up in the crowd, sirens blaring; the dog wounded Joan Jones when, as she knelt at its side to provide aid and comfort, it scratched her face badly with a wild, blind swipe of a paw. In the main the clamor was overwhelming for all involved. Virginia's arm would never fully recover from this attack. She would spend months in physical therapy.

Rolando visited her in the hospital immediately after the unexpected rampage, of course, and she was surprised at how this went. He said he didn't want to see her anymore.

"But why?"

"Virginia...you have some qualities I love. You're the only woman I've ever dated who could dress herself with her back to the mirror. You're smart, funny, accomplished. But you're oblivious to some critical realities – and I can't be with someone like that."

"What critical realities? What are you talking about?"

This was a semi private room; the person on the other side of the curtain began to groan audibly as Rolando spoke. The curtain was drawn, and by sound alone it was hard to tell if the groan was male or female.

Rolando held her hand in both of his; she was lying in the bed, he sitting in the chair next to it. "I've been thinking about the incident with Plowfinger. 'Fuck him' was what you said when I said you shouldn't have flaunted me in his face."

"It's still what I say today, now, this minute."

He fell back in the chair and sighed. The groaning on the other side of the room became more pronounced, more emphatic, more like a howl of the dead in a cheap film.

Virginia was doing all she could to keep from moaning out loud herself. Every few seconds the powerful clamping jaws of the dog kept flashing before her eyes. She also knew, in her heart of hearts, that Rolando was probably right to bring up the way she had treated Kentuckus Plowfinger.

"Virginia – haven't you ever seen one of these shows like *Forensic Files* or *Cold Case Files?*"

"What? What does that have to do with anything? Have you gone crazy Rolando?"

"You can't push a jilted lover like that over the edge Virginia."

"Come on."

"I'm telling you Virginia. This is the kind of situation you read about in the papers all the time. A guy can't keep a job. He can't get the woman he's obsessed with. He gets humiliated by her in public, in front of other people. You understand? He hits the boiling point. You turn a lonely corner one night and there he is with a knife or a gun."

Virginia laughed. "Don't be ridiculous."

"Jealousy is one of the most destructive forces on Earth. People go insane with the desire for revenge. I didn't like that whole situation."

"Stop it. You're being ridiculous."

"It's not ridiculous. It's not."

A nurse appeared to say Rolando had to leave, that doctors wanted to see Virginia for some tests. Rolando stood up and kissed Virginia on the forehead gently, a goodbye forever love peck. He stood over her a moment, still holding her hand in both of his. "I'll call you later," Virginia said.

"No. Don't."

"Rolando –"

"Goodbye Virginia. Don't call me."

"We can talk this out a little more no?"

"Sir," the nurse said gently. She looked half dead, half asleep, worn out. "I really must ask you to leave. I must get her ready. The doctor will be here in a moment."

Rolando left without another word or another look back. As he walked out Virginia saw him from the back, wiping his shocky lock out of his eyes.

Virginia lay back, in pain, waiting. The bewails from the other bed were a steady stream now. Virginia wondered what the ailment was but the finality of Carspidrain's behavior immediately wiped that out. The nurse stood there writing on a chart. The other patient in the room moaned and groaned more and more loudly, then their silhouette could be seen through the curtain trying to rise up from the bed. The disgusting smell of hospitals – a fusion of medicinal chemicals and dirty bodies – was pungent in Virginia's mind. The roommate wobbled, convulsed, shook, and fell to the floor with a gigantic crash, apparently knocking over a bedside tray. The patient screamed. The nurse ran over to help while Virginia, her arm on fire with pain by now, lay there thinking about the possibility of someday having to confront Kentuckus Plowfinger with a knife or a gun.

Burn Series

"Viagra for women was invented a long, long time ago. It's called money."

Dixie Demando was in bed alone, asleep, at four AM when she heard this remark in the front vestibule of her apartment. She groaned, smiled, and rolled over with half conscious appreciation for the humor. Her alarm clock went off at five thirty every weekday morning; she habitually hit the snooze about fourteen times before exiting the pallet. If the noisemaking guests had come in so loudly at, say, two, she might have caracoled up and made an issue of the clamor but, hey, an hour and a half wasn't all that bad.

As she always did in the dreamy reverie of morning she hugged her extra pillow and thought hungrily of The Boy. The Boy, with his cell phone and headphones, probably uploading pics onto Instagram.

Dixie Demando had a halcyon, congenial reverse commute that the masses and throngs would envy – she took the ferry *from* Manhattan *to* Staten Island at eight AM, the opposite of what tens of thousands of other commuters had to do each day. The ride was her smooth and peaceful intermezzo before the insanity of her work life and, similarly on the way back in the evening, before the riotous hullabaloo of her personal life.

An example of the febrile babel of said personal life might be this: her sister Kim was in from San Diego. In the weeks leading up to her visit all of Kim's texts and emails revolved around one theme: the price of New York hotels. She finally stopped beating around the bush and got right down to it. "Dixie, I can't afford it. Can I stay with you?" Dixie was disgusted. She wished her sister could just present her gold digging without such obvious attempts to edulcorate. Kim didn't work; somehow she survived off men. Her Facebook was page was a life album of herself in bikinis and provocative outfits, surrounded by other likeminded girls and studly young guys with chiseled pecs and tattoos. She hadn't had a real job in years, always claiming poverty on her tax returns and listing her occupation as a waitress. She had a food stamp card and Gucci bags. She drove up to the offices of government assistance agencies in her Infiniti G37x. When that car wasn't available to her in southern California, on public buses, when she wanted to change out of stiletto heels and into the comfy Keds she carried in her bag, whatever young man was accompanying her was expected to kneel down and execute the change.

Twice, as a young adult, she had come to Dixie for money for abortions. Dixie told her there would be no third time. Now and then Dixie suspected Kim had been in trouble with the police but nothing ever came of that either. The difference in their lives and personalities was unfathomable to Dixie, who took after their parents – industrious and motivated, ambitious and hard working. Kim was even different insofar as she was a blonde – everybody else in the family had dark hair, not only their parents but all the aunts and uncles and cousins, everybody. It was as if nature wanted to differentiate her by appearance as well as personality.

Kim, however, was not without her strong points. For example, she had a rare aptitude for foreign languages and was three quarters of the way fluent in four of them – Spanish, Arabic, Russian, and Chinese. Amazing! People's mouths dropped open when they heard her speaking these tongues – it was so surprising to hear them coming out of her mouth, this Venus in shredded jeans. Still, Dixie had long, long ago prophesized to herself that Kim's life would end in ruins. She hoped not, against all of her intuitions.

It was Kim who had smashed into the apartment at four, with two gentlemen quite a bit younger than herself in suits, gripping bottles of champagne by the necks, talking loudly and incoherently, trying to sing, Kim's glasspaper throaty laughter punctuating the unintelligible rambling of her escorts. They immediately went into the guest bedroom and slammed the door shut behind them as crassly as they had done the front door when they came in. The talk and laughter went on for a few moments and then there was total silence.

Four oh five AM – Dixie Demando thinks wonderfully swooning thoughts of The Boy. Maybe today would be the day she finally went up to him and started a conversation. *Excuse me, I see you almost every day and I thought perhaps we should introduce ourselves. I'm Dixie...*

Every morning when Dixie disembarked from the (mostly empty) ferry that brought her from Manhattan to Staten Island she walked through the terminal, passing the crowds upon crowds upon crowds of people waiting to board a Manhattan bound boat. Many of the same faces were recognizable to her each day, people going to the city to work, to school, to jobs they hated, to jobs they loved, to classes they feared, to classes they enjoyed, to court, to destiny – but the one her eyes hungrily searched for, and found, was The Boy, a young man in his twenties always in an impeccable dark suit, white shirt, paisley tie, temperamental air, pouty lips, the Montgomery Clift of Wall Street. Oh! The dreamy, moody eyes, the high forehead, the limber, athletic body – this kid was the first young man who ever, *ever,* whipped up a kind of Cougartown fever inside Dixie. How many times had she silently rehearsed an approach...

Her cell phone on the nightstand next to her bed made the little musical tone it did when a text message first arrived. She felt in the dark for the phone. It was a text from her current principal squeeze, Austin Pishikaff, a lifer in the State Department. He was leaving the following day for the Middle East. He was a diplomat, a satyr, and a member of the restaurant cognoscenti. He existed on a first name basis in thirty different capital cities around the world. "Austin from Boston" was how he might be greeted by officials in Paris or in Jakarta. (It was an internationally perpetuated myth that he was a Boston native – he approved of the rhyme and never corrected the false impression.) He was a leading theoretician in Washington, a major exponent of the idea that prominence in the New World Order was no longer simply a function of military might and brute force and power. He lectured to foreign policy clubs and think tanks about complex subjects such as Modern Threat.

"Modern Threat?" Dixie laughed the first time she heard this. "Like Spanish One or Advanced Algebra? Modern Threat?" She had rolled her eyes. By way of response Pishikaff had taken her by the wrist and gently guided her hand between his legs, underneath his diplomat's trench coat, in the back seat of the NYC taxi cab, and rested her fingers around his hard on, furious beneath his trousers.

His text read:

Dixie Demando – are we gonna go commando?

They slightly amended, within the opaque structure of their relationship, the usual meaning of 'go commando' – basically, for them, it meant that Dixie wouldn't wear a bra to the movies. Tomorrow was their last chance to be together for a long time. Pishikaff would rocket up from D.C. on the Acela, they would do an artsy fartsy movie at the Angelika (the theater would be empty in the morning, he would be able to get her sweatshirt up over her head and breast feed on her tits for almost the entire length of the picture), have a quick early dinner around Houston Street at someplace like Jane or Lupa, and by seven he would be back at Dulles or Ronald Reagan bound for Tel Aviv. That was his life – fuck and negotiate, negotiate and fuck. The isometrics of Modern Threat.

Dixie thought of The Boy, she read the text from Austin Pishikaff, she wished her little sister would calm down and not be such a reckless wild woman, she floated in and out of sleep for another seventy five minutes, and then her alarm clock buzzed. It buzzed a blend of soft rock and pop. It buzzed the approach to the new day. That was how she thought of it – not as the new day but as the approach to it.

She sat on the edge of the bed and stretched her arms mightily, yawned with puissance, made her way on bare feet out of the bedroom in one of Pishikaff's custom tailored Vitaliano Pancaldi shirts that he was always leaving behind, the tails of which went past her knees.

The bathroom was in the way back of the apartment. Dixie had the top floor of a three story Chelsea townhouse, a luxurious and spacious classic of the kind that New York realtors consistently referred to as 'timeless' in radio advertisements. She turned out of her bedroom, to the right, and started towards the bathroom when a hoarse, too-many-cigarettes kind of male voice behind her said quietly "Damn, you have great maps."

She jumped in fright, then relaxed as she turned to see that this must be one of the men Kim had brought home. Indeed; he was a scruffy looking little fuckball with dark, darting eyes and a deep scar virtually the entire length of his left temple; two of the fingers on his left hand were heavily bandaged with white medical tape. His white shirt and black pants, it seemed to Dixie, should have been much more wrinkled than they were. She tried to smile like a good hostess. He smiled too, without showing any teeth. "Great maps?" Dixie asked him overly questioningly, with too much emphasis.

He pointed downwards. "A woman has veins in the tops of her feet that comprise maps. Road maps." He burped drunkenly to chaperon the explanation. "Yours point to an exquisite journey."

Dixie sized him up, something she did with people all day long at her executive position. He was a hands guy, a prince of gesticulation. He had never taken a woman's virginity – no gal would ever willingly accept him as her first. This was a man who spent his whole working day on the fiftieth floor, looking out over the city between frantic, urgent calls from his desk phone. When he got off work at six it was hard for him to adjust to dealing with people on the ground, people who experience the world at ground level all day long. He was probably making money but, equally probably, he was the kind of moneymaker that writers like Drieser or McInerney would desire to skewer. Dixie noted the pack of menthol cigarettes in his breast pocket. Lastly she observed how vitreous his eyeballs were.

"Oooooohhhhh kaaaaay." Dixie smiled again, holding out her hand. "Hi. I'm Dixie Demando, Kim's sister. This is my apartment."

He shook her hand. "Buck Wiscusaprig. Pleased to meet you. I would say I've heard a lot about you but I haven't. I have no idea who you are or what I'm doing here. Your sister is in bed with my friend in there, that next room there. You look like you have to pee."

"Well –"

"Don't flush the toilet to camouflage the sound of the pee tinkling in the bowl, please. Don't start my day with that kind of falsehood."

Dixie laughed and made her way to the bathroom, and when she urinated she complied with his request. Exiting the bathroom she asked Buck, "Are Kim and –"

"McGeorge."

"Are Kim and McGeorge asleep?"

"Oh, like babies. Let's take a peek."

"Umm..."

"Don't worry Dixie, they're decent. They're dressed, actually. Fell asleep in their clothes."

"Let me see." She stuck her head in the door of the guest room to behold McGeorge and Kim out cold, back to back, wholly dressed, mouths open like pigs on a spit. She began to close the door softly, trying to be quiet; it creaked on its hinges. At the last split second before the door closed, however, in the corner of the room she noticed something odd – a small portable pet cage. She did a double take, then indicated it to Wiscusaprig with a nod of her head. "What's that?" she whispered. "Do you know what that is?"

He put his finger to his lips and put his hand on top of hers to complete the physical action of closing the door. Then he met her stunned gaze of curiosity with "That's McGeorge's kitty cat and its clone."

"What? Clone?"

"Sure. You know how it is. McGeorge, your sister, and I are what people in Antonioni's day used to call the idle rich. McGeorge's parents paid thirty thousand dollars to have his pussycat cloned. It was such a festive occasion back in the day. Do we have coffee, Dixie?"

While she digested the information about uninvited animals in her apartment she said "Yes, give me a moment, I'll make some," and then darted into her bedroom to tug on a pair of black leggings underneath the shirt. Pishikaff, she saw, had sent another text:

Dixie Demando – I'm caught in your quicksando.

Dixie smiled. She fully realized that all males were basically sex crazed cavemen but Austin's zeal in this regard was so over the top it seemed surreal. 'Quicksand' was his term for that special part of a woman – which wasn't bad, since she had once had a gentleman caller who referred to it as her 'hoo ha'. Yet, for all his man of the world posturing, his airs of being an urbane and debonair dandy, he really wasn't that good at either the art of romance or at physical love. He had no fluency of mobility in sex; instead, what he performed upon her was a kind of spastic heave-fuck that suggested the action, for him, was a strenuous kind of toil.

"Come, Bucky, let's have some breakfast." She felt safe and comfortable with him, perhaps unreasonably so given her complete lack of hard, tangible knowledge of anything about him. She was going by her guesstimations.

"I don't remember asking you to call me Bucky. My name is Buck."

"Did your parents baptize you Buck, or is that a nickname?"

"I wish I had my birth certificate to show you."

As they walked down the hallway to the kitchen he pointed to a picture of her maternal grandfather that she kept hanging on the wall out of a sense of familial loyalty and obligation. "Who's this meatface biohazard on the wall here?"

Dixie oscillated between laughter and anger as she started to make the coffee. Again – as she did when she ignored the loud entrance of the three earlier – she made the deliberate conscious decision that the class move was to ignore. "Some breakfast, Bucky? I usually have some fruit and melba toast."

"No bacon and eggs? Pancakes and maple syrup?" She could see he was tiring, the long night of partying catching up with him. His eyeballs were rolling of their own volition.

"No, sorry."

"Wanna see my fiancé?"

"Sure." She timed the speaking of the syllabic word with her finger clicking on the coffee maker. In spite of everything the fiancé business piqued her curiosity. They sat down together at Dixie's kitchen table. His eyes were now half shut. While he went through his phone to find pictures of his girlfriend Dixie watched in silence. The sound of the coffee maker was all that broke the quiet.

"Here," Buck Wiscusaprig said proudly. "The love of my life. Mei Wong." He held the phone towards Dixie so she could see, but it was awkward, like someone pushing a crucifix towards a vampire to repel attack.

The head shot of Mei Wong revealed wistful, melancholy beauty – a dryad in a moment of sadness, eyes looking right into the camera. Her features were perfectly delineated, delicate, her skin fruit-smooth, elaborate earrings dangling. These were a kind of earring very few women could get away with and not look utterly ridiculous in. Though there was a flower in her hair it was clearly not a staged photograph – the background was what looked like a street in the Meat Packing District. The flower was the result of a spontaneous action – Buck's? Was it Buck who took the picture? Her beauty was completed by a few streaks of bold blonde on one side of her jet black hair, more a statement than an aesthetic quality: *I can get away with it.*

"She's very beautiful," Dixie said honestly. "Wow." Buck looked crestfallen. "When's the wedding?"

"Mei's in a lot of trouble. I – she – she's almost certainly going to go to jail. I don't think our marriage is going to happen after all."

"Coffee?"

"Please. Thank you."

"What kind of trouble?"

"Here I was the last couple of years thinking she was a legitimate entrepreneur…"

"Cream and sugar?"

"No, black."

"Here you go."

"Thanks."

"Entrepreneur?"

"Yeah but, um, she's going to go to prison. She's being extradited back to China."

"I'm so sorry. For what?"

Buck slumped in the chair, sipping coffee with two hands. Whatever booze and drugs his system was jammed up with were beginning to overwhelm him. "Turns out she was the Western link in a gang in China that has been selling rat meat as lamb all over the country."

Dixie blinked. She took the phone and looked once again at the face of the nonpareil of global exotica. "Rat meat passed off as lamb?"

Buck burped again, grotesquely, and his eyes swelled up. "Yeah. They coated the flesh of the rats with gelatin and some kind of pigment and –"

Dixie held up a hand. "All right, enough. I don't really need the play by play."

"All our plans up in smoke. Dreams, my dreams…" His head slumped on the table and he wept, softly. In a moment or two he was out cold, asleep.

Dixie stared at the photo of Mei Wong while she ate her ate breakfast. Mei Wong, evidently, of the velvet hammer.

Buck's head snapped up once while she ate. "Do you have a boyfriend?" he asked dazedly.

"Yes, of course."

"What's he like?"

"He wants to retire to Bologna and cavort with the female descendants of the Maserati brothers."

At this his head hit the table once more with a thud, and then he was as good as dead. Dixie ate, swilled some coffee, and left him there while she went to shower and get dressed. A monster day of work awaited her at the office.

As the water ran over her body she theorized about The Boy. Dixie had a bit of education in various techniques of working the stock market – she envisioned her ideal lover using The Meter Drop, or perhaps Dogs of the Dow; she carried on with the exfoliating loofah sponge and imagined herself giving The Boy a massage while he explained to her the ins and outs of the miracle of Dollar Cost Averaging. She could practically feel her hands kneading the skin around his shoulder blades…

Someone else was in the bathroom.

"Hey!" Dixie called, sticking her head out around the shower curtain. "Hey! Who are you! Who's there?"

A tall, thin, wiry man-child carrying the pet cage - McGeorge regarded her with obvious embarrassment. "I'm McGeorge," he croaked. "I'm Kim's friend. I know you're showering but I just couldn't wait." He sat on the bowl in enormous haste and let rip an aeriform shot of feces that was absolutely ghastly. The two kittens in the cage jumped in fright.

"God!" Dixie cried, putting her arm in front of her face as if for protection.

McGeorge asked meekly, "Did you ever see the movie *Armageddon?*"

"What?"

He repeated, "Did you ever see the movie *Armageddon?*"

"No. Why?" she snapped the shower curtain back across her face.

"It's playing in your toilet bowl right now."

"Will you finish up and get the hell out of my bathroom please?" Now she was starting to get hot under the collar, her poise and patience slipping. This kid McGeorge reeked of booze in a way that Buck had not.

"Take it easy miss high and mighty, OK? Would you rather I just shit in your extra bed? In your hallway?"

"Get out!" Dixie yelled, and he staggered out.

When she was done with her shower she saw that he had left the cage with the cats behind. She sat on the edge of the bathtub and observed.

Their indiscerniblity, down to the whiskers, was utterly remarkable. It was scary, really. They peered back at her with lazy curiosity, then got bored and began to lick themselves.

"Do you know," McGeorge was in the doorway, "what we went through to clone these cats?"

"Listen," Dixie said, annoyed because he had a beer in his hand, one he had pilfered from her refrigerator. "I'm getting angry. I think you and your friend Buck had better leave now. Collect him and go please."

He smiled. He was a fair skinned red headed, freckled like a teenager and obviously an utter mess. He indicated the cats in the cage with the beer bottle. "Can you guess their names?"

"Heckle and Jeckle."

"Rosencrantz and Guildenstern."

"That's nice. Listen. You're a strange man in my bathroom at six o'clock in the morning drinking a beer –"

"You wanna do some lines? I have."

"– and I'm old enough to be your mother and I'm wrapped in a towel. This is not a good prescription."

"So?"

"What do you mean, so?"

"So tell your sister not to pick up men at black tie events and bring them home."

"Ugh! What kind of event was it?"

"It was an opening reception for an artist at an art gallery. Not far from here, actually. Although we ended up at six or seven clubs before we came home."

Home. "Well – get out please? I need to get dressed and go to work."

"You know that two cloning companies we were set up with went out of business before we could get it done?" He nodded toward the cats. "That's how long we had to wait."

Amazingly, right here he gave a cultured little speech about how artists and galleries were leaving Chelsea for Los Angeles in droves. Dixie knew about this; was interested in the issue; had opinions about it; did not want to discuss it with this punk.

"I think you're pathetic. I think you carry your cloned cats around for attention. I think it's ridiculous. Now get the hell out of my bathroom, please." She saw that there were three or four loose cigarettes and a book of matches in his breast pocket, which was a problem. A wealthy kid like this (his first car, at seventeen, a Porsche) should be firing up cigarettes with an expensive gold lighter, not ordinary matches. Dixie studied him while he stood there. He oozed the sheltered innocence of the insanely rich from every pore and every other hole in his body. His was face was peach fuzz clean – what, had he shaved somewhere at two AM? He was all forehead. His hairline wasn't receding, but whenever it started to his head would look gigantic and his parents would find some surgeon who could be handsomely compensated to correct it. Unlike his friend Buck, in high school he had been a cherry popper. Not because of himself but because of his parents' wealth. Their statues and marble floor and gilded staircases had gotten this child all the pussy he could wag his pathetic pecker at.

Thus scolded, bitter, he took the cats and left, swilling beer thirstily.

"Modern diplomacy," Pishikaff had lectured to a rather large group the one time Dixie had gone to hear him, "has its own best practices, and one of them is to follow the maxim of the great hypermodern chess master Nimzovich. Does anyone know what the principle is? Any serious chess players here tonight?" No one moved. Nothing stirred. You couldn't hear a whisper in the hall. "The principle is," Pishikaff said at the podium, pausing, "that the threat is sometimes stronger than the execution."

The topic of the symposium was Getting China to Put Sanctions on Iran, but Dixie noticed that this was a principle that Austin From Boston applied strategically in his own personal relationships as well as geopolitically - both with her and with others, for example his cranky octogenarian parents. She thought about this in the minutes after McGeorge went off and fell asleep again next to Kim. And when Dixie was finished in the bathroom and returned to her bedroom to get dressed there was a third text from him.

Dixie Demando — my consciousness expando.

Paused at her dresser, Dixie went through her journal. She had once heard about a speaker named Peter Daniels, an Australian businessman who was said to have read over five hundred biographies of famous men and women. This had seemed to her to be excellent training for living life, and she took up this reading habit in conjunction with another, one that she learned from Bellow's Herzog – writing letters to famous dead people. She wrote letters to those whose biographies she had read or was reading. She stood there for a moment reviewing her letter of the day before.

> *Dear Ava Gardner:*
>
> *What a life you lived. I often wonder how many relationships like yours and Frank's there are around me every day – a lot, I think. But I wonder if your easy mastery of men wasn't also your downfall, in a way. When I read that you had gone to bed with Fidel Castro I understood fully the power of a woman, of her beauty, of her capabilities.*
>
> *Ava - in your autobiography you wrote, or your ghostwriters wrote, of a black boy you were friends with when you were a little girl in North Carolina, your friend Shine. One day he went away for good and you never saw him again in your life, but as you were composing your memoirs you wrote that so many years later you still remembered him and loved him. I have a man in life with whom, I suspect, I am going to create a similar situation. I don't even know his name, but I think of him as The Boy.*

"Dix?"

Dixie stiffened at the sound of her sister's voice behind her. She didn't turn but instead looked to the mirror. Kim was in the doorway in a bra and panties, evidently having tugged off the clothes she had fallen asleep in, quite appealing in the clarity of her debauchery. Her voice was like sandpaper.

"What is it Kim?"

"Dixie listen. Don't hate me."

"I don't hate you. I'm just disappointed."

"Then don't be disappointed. Can you not be negative toward me?"

"Kim – what are you doing with your life? Look at you, running around with these worthless boys."

"Do I have to go outside to smoke? Dixie – your hair is almost silver. It looks like a fiber optic Christmas tree."

"Yes. Outside."

"Can I just climb out on the fire escape?"

Dixie closed her journal, put it in a locked drawer, and gave a disgusted wave of her arm. "Sure, go ahead. I have to get ready for work."

"You go to work so early?"

"Eight. I stop at the gym in Staten Island right by my office before I go in for the day. I shower there."

"Where are your suits? You go to work in business suits, don't you? You carry those on the ferry boat?"

"If you have to know Kim, on Monday mornings I take a car in with my five suits in garment bags and on Friday evening I take a car home with them."

"A car. You mean a limo picks you up."

"Yes Kim. Do you want to smoke? Let me give you a plastic cup with some water in it to use as an ashtray."

They laughed together at Dixie's impulse to take car of Kim, to see that she was comfortable – this always won out over anger, always had since they were children. As they walked to the kitchen Kim (the taller of the two) rested her head on Dixie's shoulder like a child. "I've been having an online affair with McGeorge for about six months. He wants to marry me."

"Every man you take to the cleaners wants to marry you baby, what's new?"

"He came out to San Diego twice on his father's private jet."

"Oh yeah?"

"Yeah. He flew me to the Yellowstone Club."

"Kim, do you think I was born yesterday?"

Kim seized Dixie's arm to indicate seriousness. "I'm not kidding you Dixie. His father is a member of the Yellowstone Club."

Dixie whistled softly. Could it possibly be true?

Kim was up on the kitchen countertop, opening the window, squeezing through it to get out on the fire escape and smoke. It was going to be a glorious day.

"So what does he do? Work for his father?"

"Well – he's trying to open an ideation company. To sell his ideas. You know, like BrightHouse?"

Dixie didn't know, and said so. "Ideas? Like cloning rabbits?"

Kim blew smoke; Dixie could hear the sucking of her breath. All she could see of Kim were her ankles and feet. "I know what you think, that he's just some stupid rich punk completely dependent on his father for everything."

"Something like that, yeah. To be frank."

"He has some great ideas."

"Like what?"

Kim tapped ashes into the makeshift ashtray. "Right now he's working on a tornado rejection catapult."

"A tornado rejection catapult."

"Right."

"Kim – what is a tornado rejection catapult?"

"Well – you know when you see those twisters out in the Midwest?"

"Yes?"

"And you can actually see it, see the shape of it, in the sky?"

"Yes?"

"McGeorge wants to assemble a team of engineers and architects to build a huge catapult to catch the twister and repel it."

"Repel it?"

"Yeah! Throw it back where it came from."

"Kim –"

"It will save thousands of lives!"

"Baby –"

"And that's just one of his amazing ideas."

"And that's just one of his amazing ideas," Dixie repeated sarcastically. She wondered if Kim was serious, if she knew had to mithridate herself from herself, from her own tendencies and game playing with the world at large. Unfortunately she suspected not.

Dixie was thinking, as she had thought many times in her life, that her sister had perfect feet. She had perfect everything. Even now, as she lifted her feet to swing them through the window first, and Dixie could see that the bottoms of them were filthy from the fire escape, they were perfect. Some people were just born with it.

Once inside Kim seemed to have succumbed – like her pals Buck Wiscusaprig and McGeorge – to the amount of drugs and alcohol she had consumed overnight. "How come you never come out to San Diego to visit me Dixie? I have a great apartment in the Gaslamp Quarter. My boyfriend is the conductor of the San Diego Symphony."

Dixie burst out laughing in spite of it all. "What does McGeorge think about your boyfriend? Or vice versa?"

Kim gave a knowing, ugly, drunken smile. Dixie escorted her into bed next to the snoring McGeorge. Buck Wiscusaprig was still asleep at the kitchen table.

Dixie put on her gym sweats, sneakers, collected her bag, and went out to meet the day. She loved her neighborhood, Chelsea. There was always something new to observe, for example a sign with a mock stop sign on it: STOP BEDBUGS! CHINCHAS! WWW.BEDBUGKING. COM . Or these Body Work massage parlors that were springing up everywhere in the five boroughs these days – were they fronts for Chinese prostitutes? Delivery trucks, double parked, with wild pop art painted all over their panels; old church spires rising towards the sky – the churches were practically nothing but museums now. A public park named for a slain police officer: PO DAVID WILLIS BASKETBALL COURT. She walked to Broadway and got on the R train to Whitehall Street to catch the ferry. She wondered, for the umpteenth time in her life, why she just didn't take her employers' offer of a town car to take her to work via Jersey, the Lincoln tunnel, the Bayonne Bridge. The answer she gave herself was always the same – she liked to be among the people in the streets, in the subways, on the ferry.

She saw that another text from Pishikaff had come in but she didn't read it right away. To text her four times before seven AM meant that he was desperate about something. She smiled inwardly, remembering him working with the European Union and Greenpeace protestors about genetically modified corn made by a company named Syngenta. The Greenpeace people had come to protest with a huge anthropomorphic cob of corn with a greedy evil smile on its face. This had been her introduction to his seriocomic world, about eight years previous.

Boarding the boat her mind began to come alive with the anticipation of seeing The Boy. She took a seat outside, facing Brooklyn, closing her eyes for a moment, turning her face up to the morning sky, feeling the sea air in her lungs, conscious of, but not looking at, the golden swath of sunrise that Staten Island is bathed in at this hour of the morning on this kind of day. Her back was to the Statue of Liberty, to the Bayonne Bridge, to New Jersey.

On the boat, her eldritch life on hold for the twenty minute ride, she rehearsed the introduction in her mind again. *Hi, I'm Dixie, nice to meet you. And your name is?*

This was the water of heaven, of baptisms - a rich, deep blue on such a day, Not perfect water by any means of course, not the glasslike surface of a tropical beach, not a diaphanous jewel, not Tiberias, but the strong blue waves that were the confident forces of nature that had inspired the poets for centuries. She observed the boats and ships that sat motionless in the water between Staten Island and Brooklyn – freighters, cargo ships, trawlers – waiting to be admitted into port. Two sportsmen on little speed boats, clad in frogman suits, zipped along, racing each other, almost as far away as the eye could see toward the Brooklyn side. Deep in the distance, coming towards the very boat she was on, she could see, under the Verrazano Bridge, a cruise ship that she had been observing about every two weeks for years, coming to land in Jersey, bringing home a ship full of exhausted party animals.

Such a fine day it already was. *Excuse me, I thought since we see each other practically every day we might as well say hello. My name is Dixie...*

On her cell phone – still ignoring the last text from Austin Pishikaff – she played around with a memo to herself, a rough couple of notes for the next letter she wanted to try to compose in her journal later in the evening:

> *Dear Katherine Hepburn:*
>
> *(Write something about "Box Office Poison" and her magnificence in The Philadelphia Story; the pictures with Spencer Tracy; the heartbreak of On Golden Pond; and more.)*

That one would need a lot of work. The letters that she would leave behind, after her death, in her journals were of the utmost importance to Dixie – they had to be the best that she could make them. They were going to be her legacy. She had a lot of money that she was going to leave to a lot of charities but her journals were going to be her legacy.

She put her phone in her pocket and meditated to the soft purr of the boat's engines cutting through the water. Two Scandinavian couples speaking in their native languages came and sat nearby, smiling pleasantly, snapping photos, leafing through some tourist brochures. A homeless man that Dixie recognized from years of riding the ferry shuffled by, smelling awful and looking worse. Some people spend thirty grand on cloning kittens, some people scam an entire nation (the biggest nation on Earth) about what they're eating, some people drag themselves around a ferry boat looking in the garbage cans for scraps. Dixie was wise enough to know she would never be able to figure any of it out.

She felt and heard the phone vibrating in her pocket. In the intervening seconds between the moment that she first heard it and the moment that she saw the name on the phone's screen she surmised to herself that it was either Kim, calling to ask where she could find some particular thing in the apartment, or else it was one of the early birds at her office asking her to authorize a decision they themselves were too scared to make.

Neither – it was Joe Smith, the property manager of her building.

"Hello? Joe?"

"Ms. Demando, yes it's Joe Smith."

"What a surprise. What's up?"

"Ms. Demando, something terrible – your apartment is going up in flames. There's a fire in your apartment. Ms. Demando? Are you there? Is there anyone in the apartment? Ms. Demando?'

The Exousia

Initially, in the hours right after his death, all anybody knew about him for certain was that he was murdered in a shockingly unusual fashion in a Pacific Coast League baseball stadium. First inquiries uncovered rumors of an association with a woman who had connections to a minor league club that didn't play in that league, the Lansing Lugnuts, but she was never found. Also among the preliminary impressions were indications of an uncle who was very prominent in Plaid Cyrmu – another dead end. He had no cell phone on his body and no known Instagram account.

In the aftermath of sensational deaths numerous post mortem facts, of course, never stop pouring out. This one produced an anabasis of such. A woman who had seen the dead man's face plastered all over Facebook came forward to offer the following. She had sat next to him once on a flight from San Francisco back to Boston. She, the witness, was a well prepared traveler. She had equipped herself with two homemade sandwiches that she brought on board, not content to fly six hours on the bag of peanuts provided by the airline. She ate a sandwich and a half and allowed the other uneaten half to rest on the tray table unfinished, waiting for an attendant to collect it. Wild - the dead man had asked her if he could have it. Her story was backed up by a check of the records – indeed, they had sat together on the flight. But so what? She had no other news about him.

The police found problems with his bank accounts. For example, there wasn't any money in them.

They found problems with him medically – he consistently ignored his prescriptions for Metformin and Onglyza. Should he have expected positive results from this behavior?

A second female came forward to volunteer this information: she and a former boyfriend, a shady character in his own right, had met the dead man in a bus station in some Godforsaken town in Texas. The bus came through about once every six hours. To amuse themselves the three of them played the Battleship app on their cell phones together. The rough guy, the boyfriend, had been greatly amused by the dead man's rank in the game – Seaman. "Ha ha, look at you – Seaman!" Perhaps he thought seaman was semen, who can say? The police thanked this second lady but her story couldn't be corroborated at all.

A third person, a man eighty years of age, presented himself to report that the deceased one had been an orderly in a Boston hospital where he had once been a patient. The old man, coherent if a little shaky, claimed to recall an incident with great vividness and distinction. The dead man had come around taking lunch orders between the hospital ward's various groans and screams. He offered a choice of pork or salmon, writing the orders down on a little card. The old man had asked, "What kind of pork is it?"

"I don't know," was the answer from the dead. Then, uselessly, he threw in "Cooked pork." It was a tale again confirmed: the murdered had indeed worked at the hospital. But once more the question came: so what?

People – adults in their twenties – recalled seeing the dead hombre in New York years before – any time a new type of sneaker was released and New York kids camped out all night in front of Foot Locker, etc., so as to be able to be the first to make the purchase at 6AM – he was there. There were dozens of photos of him on these footwear lines, soon to be as viral as all get out. This triggered many, many soul searching articles in the mainstream press along the lines of Why Are These Kids Camping Out All Night To Spend $225 On Sneakers? Little was seen in terms of analyzing the heaps of garbage, feces, beer cans, rivers of urine, uneaten food, broken cheap beach chairs, vomit, used up condoms, etc, that these All Americans left on the public thoroughfares of their nation in their wake. Why was the victim such a fervent sneaker boy? Why? Oh why? Amazingly, an old article turned up in which the featured deceased was interviewed about sneakers:

> "And with pairs of the awesome sneakers already being
> sold on eBay for as much as $660 dollars, it's not hard to

see why someone would camp out all night in order to buy this shoe, which retails for only $180 dollars.

"I can turn around and flip them online and make myself a couple hundred for the holidays," this shopper said on Thursday, while waiting patiently for Foot Locker to reopen at 7 a.m., Friday, in order to pick up his new pair of Jordans.

Although, for this shopper and company, camping out for a "fresh set of kicks," as they put it was all about looking "fly," another way of saying "good."

"It's a lifestyle," said fellow shopper Millicent Swankpee, one of the few females in the group.

Then a woman somewhat known in Boston society, one Victoria Spaniffiquaze, leapt forth with more. This man, said she, had been one of the crew who washed the awning of her apartment building on Boylston, right across from the Public Garden, every Sunday morning. Various of the principals rubbed their chins- even if this was true, why would Victoria Spaniffiquaze bring it out? Seasoned law enforcement professionals speculated as to her motive. Was this merely dutiful citizenship?

"I will never forget him," she astoundingly declared.

"Why?"

"You know my car. I have a Volkswagen Eos. E-O-S."

"Yes?"

"He would call it an Eso. E-S-O. Eso. Ease oh. He said it hundreds of times. Eso, Eso. I wanted to rip his tongue out of his mouth! I wanted to slap his face!"

It was soon understood that none of Victoria Spaniffiquaze's various accounts had any merit. Her stories had more hair on them than a barbershop. She was exposed as an evil adulteress, and a jaywalker. She had never owned any kind of Volkswagen, Eos or otherwise. She had no credibility whatsoever. She and her poodle, which was named Blue Sofisticato, habitually trampled on the grass in the Public Garden, ignoring all rules and posted signs. And the worst about her was yet to come. In the most recent election of a Pope in Rome, when Francis of South America was chosen, this Spaniffiquaze woman had disguised herself in one layer as a man, then in another layer as a Bishop of the Church, and had sneaked into the College of Cardinals, fooling the Swiss Guards who manned a Security Station with her outfit and bogus credentials from a non existent entity called the Italian Orthodox Church and a false religious order. Alas, she made mistakes –

Her cassock was too short and she wore a Fedora rather than the standard skull cap. But she had brazenly bullshitted her way into the election of the Pope!

Before the case was thrown into the Cold Case files for eternity, however, there were several more developments of note. It seemed that the dead man had kept some kind of diary or journal, fragments of which were found. The first (authenticated) excerpt to appear on the internet read as such:

> "All who read this will see my torcha. How I was pushed to the edge!! Hayzahoona is the boss. The landlord, the boss, the property owner, the cheese. BastiCocco is an employee of his and so am I. Hayzahoona owns the whole street. I don't know what you call them, red brick houses, three apartments in each, in Chicago we would call them three-flats but I don't know the Boston name. He owns the whole side of the street, 26 buildings, on the facing side he owns 19. They're less on that side cuz their 4 or 5 lil shops on the end of the block that never make it. One week its a hare place and the next time you look its a pet shop. Lucille used to get her hare done in the place that became something diffrent."

Linus BastiCocco sang like a canary, though the property magnate Hayzahoona was harder to get statements from. BastiCocco served as the super and handyman for the nineteen buildings on one side of the South End street. The dead man performed the same function for the twenty six. Each drew the same salary from Hayzahoona, but by way of compensation for having more buildings and apartments to look after the dead man was given a rent free apartment (on another street).

BastiCocco informed the authorities that the dead handyman was having trouble with a neighbor – upstairs, in the apartment over his – and the neighbor's constantly barking dog. This miniature terrier was barely larger than a healthy rat but it barked its head off day and night. The dead man tied to reason with the dog owner, an emaciated and elderly lady named Toyami who didn't say much other than "Your fuckin' culo."

"Can I have a word with you please?"

"A word? About what?"

"Your dog's barking."

"Your fuckin' culo."

Now the apartment given the dead fellow by his employer Hayzahoona was in a row of ivy colored red brick buildings overlooking the Massachusetts Turnpike, obviously a block that throbbed with the roar of traffic day and night. The dead one was seen numerous times pleading with the half crippled Toyami, who stood there with her little dog on a leash and listened irritably but never did anything about the barking. Incredibly, none of the other neighbors – neither adjacent nor above – seemed to mind the barking much. BastiCocco knew this because the deceased had brought him over to the house a couple of times to attempt to reason with the old woman, and to try to get the other neighbors to sign a petition. No go – the dead and BastiCocco had doors slammed in their faces like Robert Redford and Dustin Hoffman in *All The President's Men*. No one wanted any part of it. One man explained it thus:

"That Toy? No man, I don't want nothin' to do with that crazy bitch. She'll put a dead rooster outside my door. She'll sprinkle goofah dust where I lay my head. She has all these flipped out potions and shit. Hoodoo candles. No thanks bro, get someone else to sign." He looked past the shoulders of the two at his door, out into the past, or perhaps the future, with the otiose eye of the defeated.

Finally the dead man, going out of his mind from the barking, blew a hundred bucks on something called "Ultimate Bark Control" a machine that humanely directed high frequency sound waves at dogs to make them stop barking – a form of mechanized behaviorism. It was guaranteed to work up to three hundred feet away or your money back. He set it up skeptically in his apartment, hooking it up horizontally at the top of a ladder, and waited for Toyami to re enter her apartment after taking the dog out for a walk (he always knew when she was returning because she slammed the door shut with high inconsideration). He crouched in wait, sweating, looking out his window at the palatial glass of the Hancock Tower fulgurating in the sunlight. Then – SLAM! Toyami and her dog came home, entering the apartment above. Immediately the dog launched into its habitual sonic routine and the dead mounted the ladder, grabbing the Ultimate Bark Control device with both hands and pointing it in the general direction of the dog's barking. After no more than ten seconds there was silence – total quiet! The dead man related to Linus BastiCocco that this break, this respite, this stoppage of the auditory torment, was like a sudden miracle. He had no words to describe it. He got a decent night's sleep for the first time in months. However the peace was not to last as the hoodoo woman Toyami would not go down so easily.

And yet from other sectors more witnesses from the life of the murdered man continued to come forward. Truly he had lived a most adventurous existence. A tattooed ruffian in a wheelchair who claimed to be a poker colleague said the dead man was well known for making sandwiches in the following manner – he would take a brand new loaf of bread, remove the end slice and dump out all the intervening slices on the table just to be able to get to the other end slice and thus make a sandwich with the two ends.

An anorexic girl with no good prospects was found and brought in – she told the investigators that she always would remember the man despite the fact that their relationship had been nothing but a short sexual collision.

"Why? Why will you always remember him?"

"He gave me this note. He stuffed it in my bra in the middle of dinner at Denny's the last time I ever saw him."

> *"The best movie ever is the The French Connector. You no why? Theirs no girl to fuck him up. Theirs no love interest. Popeye fucks a one night stand and you barely dont even see her, shes in the back of the picture in the bed room. I never saw that ever in another pickture. There always sticking some broad in in a big roll so they can have a star actress be the wife or the girlfren. Here it was just like look, he fucks her, thats all."*

Cheap Kenna Dipthong, however, was perhaps the most interesting of the dead man's ex lovers to emerge. She hailed from the River Walk in San Antonio. She was the live in girlfriend of Linus BastiCocco and her affair with the dead one had subsisted undetected for more than a year. She spoke with eloquence to the police, fueling speculation that she had once played Beatrice in a sub par production of *Much Ado About Nothing,* directed by a man now in prison for boldly exhibiting his penis to children in the subway.

"It was a beautiful crisp fall day, really the first day that you could feel autumn in the air after the heat of summer. We were walking through the Common. He pointed out to me a group of pigeons that he said he frequently saw on a little knoll near Boylston Street." The police knew the area, it was across the street from Emerson College. "He took me by the hand and we ran to a store and bought a loaf of bread and ran back and fed it to the pigeons, ripping the slices of bread up into little pieces and throwing them to the birds. He said we would go eat breakfast and then come back and see how much of the bread the pigeons had devoured." She said this silly exercise made her feel liberated, like a little girl, free, playful, full of fun and laughter, it was something Linus BastiCocco wouldn't do with her in a hundred years, skip with her across the park and in the streets in pursuit of a mysterious goal. (The best BastiCocco could ever do was take her to a movie and for a cheeseburger. Big whoop!)

Her sincerity was unquestioned, and unquestionable. Her face had its own grammar when she spoke – you believed her no matter what.

Someone produced the following information – when you Googled the name Spaniffiquaze the Google search engine asked you *Did you mean Spanish Quiz? There are no results for "Spaniffiquaze".*

All known photographs of him displayed the same icy Eurasian severity, the raw kind of lunatic animal sexuality we associate with, say, Stanley Kowlaski.

Toyami was known to have confronted the dead man, knocking on his door and screaming "Your fuckin' culo!" at the top of her lungs. She was convinced he had put some kind of hoodoo hex – her own specialty indeed – on her little dog to make it stop barking.

Cheap Kenna Dipthong continued with her account. She was, in fact, connected to The Bard but not by means of *Much Ado*; rather, she had once played Goneril for a week, taken a week off to execute a starvation diet, shed good poundage, then returned to the same production in the third week to play Regan. Haplessly, she confused some of the two sisters' lines. It was a contemporary production, somewhat arrant, spearheaded by a director of vision who thought it was hip and postmodern to have the players wear contemporary garb; to play Regan he brought Cheap Kenna Dipthong a pair of glaikit jeans that had the word PLAY spelled out on the two back pockets – PL on the left and AY on the right, except that the A was in the shape of a heart. Cheap Kenna Dipthong, a ravishing girl of great beauty, had her doubts that this was appropriate attire for Regan but she let it go since the whole production was a fucking disastrous mess anyway.

The actor who played Gloucester was a Senegalese refugee – he was onstage in the name of diversity – who had recently been in the news for having produced twenty children by thirteen different women. At first nobody connected to the play could quite believe this but lo, there was the loving father on You Tube, freely admitting to his widespread cocksmanship. One afternoon, as he was staggering about the stage with the bloody eye patches already on (it was quite deep into the performance) BastiCocco appeared screaming in the theater – he had the correct information that Cheap Kenna Dipthong was having an affair but was wrongly of the mind that the lover was the Senegalese gentleman (whom informal questioning had revealed to be the most sexually active man in all of Massachusetts). Suffice to say that this was not a pretty situation in the least. Again, while officers and agents were glad to listen, glassy eyed, to all these stories and reports there was little in the way of crime solving in them.

They returned to BastiCocco's tales of the dread Toyami.

Of a late afternoon Toyami was out walking her little terrier Jones – the pooch was always quiet when out in the streets – when who should come bouncing along but our dead friend. Below them, astride the Mass Pike, both Amtrak trains and Orange Line trains of the T were rumbling by in multiple directions. In retrospect the assumption is that he might have been coming from the theater, from the arms of Cheap Kenna Dipthong, as they were known to copulate and frolic in various broom closets there.

The dead individual hurried past, smiling with a golden inward glow, secure in the knowledge that "Ultimate Bark Control" remained firmly in his arsenal.

"Hey. Hey you. Culo!" Toyami addressed him thus. He kept going. She called after him, "Culo! It is in your best interests to speechify with me. Do not forsake me thus. Culo!"

"What is it?" He was only half turned toward her.

"What have you done to my little dog? Your fuckin' culo! To my little Jones."

"I don't know what you're talking about."

"Turn to me Culo, turn."

He turned to face the old woman, stooped over in her misery, the little dog running around happily and playfully at the end of the leash. She appeared to have barely enough strength to hold the leash. The sight of her frail, crooked frame of skin and bones might have created an imaginary chyron in his mind, imaginary commentary. The worn housedress was her habitual garment, day in and day out, she never seemed to wash it or change it or take it off – maybe she was too consumed with paresis. And yet, on her feet were brand new neon orange sandals, Adidas; her toenails looked like raptor claws. She was missing quite a number of teeth, as well.

This was all BastiCocco's account, from his memory of what the passed one had told him, and as he related it to the authorities new developments, or potential developments, were coming in all the time. The landlord Hayzahoona, heretofore reachable only through intermediaries, was now ready to talk. Additionally, a female named Elisabetta De La Real somehow emerged to further complicate the process of answering the question: who killed this man? And all the attendant questions that sprang forth therefrom.

Elisabetta De La Real was BastiCocco's mistress on the side, and the demised gentleman was in turn her lover too. Thus, the expired personnel was having simultaneous affairs with both BastiCocco's main lover and with his side lover too. (BastiCocco had been cleared of all suspicion in the case, having been vacationing at Dollywood in the Smoky Mountains when it all went down.)

Of Elisabetta De La Real let it be said: the *oomph* of Woman has rarely thus been consummated. She stated that the dead had an idiosyncrasy she well nigh dropped him over, which was this – depending on where they were, his place or hers, which hotel or motel, wherever, he had to judge the given karma or Feng shui of the given bed, the given circumstances, the given situation, to ascertain who should be on which side of the bed for sexual intercourse. At their very first meeting of love they had torn each other's clothes off like beserk animals and flown onto the mattress with abandon, fucking each other like the two parts of a crazed jackhammer, sweating, grinding, enjoying, thrusting, when he of a sudden stopped and said, "Whoa, whoa, slow down Chiquita, the shakras are all reversed."

"What?"

"Switch sides with me."

"What?"

"Switch sides of the bed."

"What? What the fuck is wrong with you? We were going at it great there."

All law enforcement officials agreed that male intuition suggested Elisabetta De La Real was probably not a chick to be fucked around with. She came at you like a Stegosaur, with plates on her back to protect yet with exposed, sexy, vulnerable sides and flanks that might really be tenderly juicy or which just might be a trap door.

She spoke of the metaphysical jealousy she could ignite at will. How had she met Linus BastiCocco? Informally, at college, they had worked together on the same student statistical research team that theorized that human birth rates went way, way up on the bell curve approximately nine months after every major blackout – in the dark, folk had little to do but some bang shang a lang. Truth be told, Elisabetta De La Real was at the forefront of this research, her probing mind leading the way, analyzing the mean, median, and mode, using innovative sampling methods, crunching numbers by a lone light long after everybody else had gone off to swill from kegs. It was an exciting time; imagine, then, her disappointment when, years after college, she ran into BastiCocco on the streets of the South End and he told her he was basically a janitor. Not that Elisabetta was anything much more, but she didn't look like that and she didn't feel like that. An idea occurred to her – in a few days she was participating in a sandwich making contest for a splendid local cause and they still needed a couple of impartial judges – why didn't BastiCocco volunteer?

He did; there was an aura about the encounter that suggested things other than sandwich making were at stake. A table was set up on a small platform behind a building and there were ample supplies of mayo, celery, carrots, and tuna fish upon it. BastiCocco sat nearby at a judges' table with three other important looking gentleman. The contestants other than Elisabetta De La Real were some slovenly two hundred pounders; Elisabetta De La Real appeared on the stage in a top that bared her midriff.

While one team of officers listened to her, another in an adjacent room got their first look at the enormously successful businessman Hayzahoona. Of him it was learned that his mother had been a participant in the world famous "Obedience to Authority" psychology experiments conducted by Stanley Milgram. She was one of those who kept pushing the shock button over and over, even when she truly believed the heinous screams she was hearing were for real. She became so grief stricken over this apparent insight into the darknesses of her own soul that she lived the rest of her life as an emotional vegetable; this had quite an impact on Hayzahoona.

Hayzahoona was completely bald but he had a hair in the dead center of his forehead that grew at an abnormal pace, faster than all the hair on the rest of his head; if a day or two went by and, due to the heat of business, he forgot to give it a snip he tended to look like a unicorn.

"So my life has been a crusade to avenge my mother."

"Avenge her against what?"

"Look – you brought me here to talk about the dead kid, right?"

"Right."

"He was a little fucked up, that kid. Great worker – a hundred times better than that other piece of shit, Bishop Cocoa."

"What do you mean?"

"I always had the feeling about him, that he was going to have a – um, a violent death."

"Why?"

"One night as I was about to get into my car – this was at my office downtown, nowhere near where he managed my buildings in the South End – he ran up to me and said there was a mistake in his paycheck."

"Yes?"

"Look, I don't like anybody to fuck with my money either, don't get me wrong. But this – this was like, fifty dollars. I mean it just wasn't that big of a deal. I remember this was a Friday afternoon – surely it could have waited till Monday."

"What did he say to you?"

"I mean these little guys, these grunts – you know, they make a living with their backs instead of their brains. Guys like me, I work with my mind not my sweat. I don't believe in manual labor. I don't trade my time for money, I trade my ideas for money. But these grunts –"

"Yes. What did he say to you?"

"It wasn't so much what he said, which I don't even remember. It was how he looked. Listen – pull it." He bent his head downwards a little, so that his chin almost pressed into his chest.

"Excuse me?"

"Pull the hair out. I see you're staring at it. The unicorn hair. Sometimes I forget to trim it."

"That won't be necessary sir. Please continue. You were saying…"

"What was I saying?"

"He ran up to you about a mistake in his paycheck?"

"Ah yes, yes. So I'm about to get into my limo to go home and he runs up to me screaming about the paycheck. The thing is, he was wearing a samurai headband, like a bandana, tied across his forehead."

"But that was not unusual for him? Mr. BastiCocco has told us this was he how he worked, habitually."

"Yeah bro, he wore standard issue bandanas, sure. But this had the rising sun and Japanese letters on it and it was so long it went all the way down to his fuckin' culo, you know what I mean?"

"So what happened?"

"I don't know, he went on jabbering about the paycheck. But he was bugged out, his eyes were wild and he was waving his arms and he was foaming at the mouth."

"Did you say foaming at the mouth?"

"Yes. He was foaming at the mouth. Frothing, like a dog. But the thing is, as soon as it happened it was done, over. He took the check and left. He went back to normal." Hayzahoona sneezed. His nose remained uncovered; a crazed wig of snot flew from it unrepentant.

To get back to another part of the overall puzzle: Elisabetta De La Real was judged by the three judges to have made the best tuna sandwiches. She won the contest. The utter charade, the complete travesty, the lowdown meanness, of judging her sandwiches to have been superior when all the contestants were making identical sandwiches out of identical ingredients right on the spot, there in front of everybody, was lost on no one. But this is life. As it happens, the man who had ceased to exist crossed paths with BastiCocco at this sandwich contest; the sneaky parties involved were able to conceal their treachery in love with still more lies.

Being one of the most confident people in the Commonwealth, Elisabetta De La Real held investigators enraptured with a tale of her childhood in the pampas. As a youngish girl, wandering through the fields, she found a cat with one of its eyes gouged out. Moved, she took it home and gave it love, attention, great affection. She loved this one eyed cat more than anything in the universe. The twisted knot of pink skin where its eye had been poked out choked her heart like nothing else in this world could, and she loved her gray and white cat more than anything, more than life itself. Sadly, a *gaucho* of bad reputation who had a venomous hatred for her father decided to exact revenge upon him (Elisabetta's dad) by seizing the beloved feline and gouging its other eye out. The method of revenge that Elisabetta exacted upon this cowboy is not suitable for description in family publications, but we may note that so many years later on, in Boston, some of the icy chill that went up detectives' spines as they questioned her could be traceable back to this incident. You just felt that her psyche was coterminous with some of the deepest evil, though in the case at hand nothing could be attributed to her.

And her high proud tits spoke of true love to be found with a man, some day, in spite of her capital mistrust of the species.

Now there was a Sino-American bus driver who drove a Huntington Avenue bus, and he was well known to some police because he had once been questioned in regard to a perversion case concerning a fetish for people who worked jobs that required them to carry things on their backs, for example leaf blowers or backpack vacuum cleaners. In that inquiry he had been immediately cleared as a suspect – the real perp had fled to Calabassas. This bus driver, Chang, came to the end of the route afternoon and was doing some Tai Chi moves in his empty bus before starting the run all over again when he noticed a bag, a small shopping bag that someone had left behind on a seat. Immediately frightened of terrorism, he called the bomb squad in.

Guess? Hoodoo candles – perfectly sculpted faces, the dead man. The credit card receipt in the bag – Toyami's. The facts: he was already dead a month but, still, these unusual candles warranted a few questions.

Toyami showed up at the police station carrying a yoga mat, a state of affairs that remained unexplained. "Many people have had children," she stated. This was evidently some kind of proleptic remark but nobody understood it.

"What?"

"Many people have had children." She clutched the yoga mat to her breast.

"You mean just in general?"

"Is that a Manduka?" asked a second officer, nodding at the yoga mat, but the first officer, senior, nudged him into silence. Toyami talked irrelevantly of how she often rode city buses wearing a derby hat and carrying a cane; when she took a seat she would take the hat off and rest it on the upright cane, which she held between her knees. With the hat removed she looked very different. The hat and cane were, like the yoga mat, props – her props for life. Her props for living life. She told the policemen that yes, she had put a spell on the expired man with her candles and other paraphernalia. Wasn't this only just, since he had put an evil hex on her little dog Jones to make it stop barking? "Ultimate Bark Control", of course, had been found in his apartment after his death. The bulls had to let Toy go – there was no law against casting hoodoo spells. It was back to square one for everyone involved.

In California a man whose DNA had been found at the scene of the crime was tracked down – it was done so because he was a career criminal, his DNA was in national law enforcement databases. Yet, since his last arrest, he had become a studious and law abiding individual, a historian who was gaining fame as one of the foremost authorities in the world on the assassination of William The Silent. What was his DNA doing at the scene of a murder though? And a murder so bizarre as this? Police had tailed him for a day before approaching him. A surveillance camera in a convenience store picked up him up buying a pack of extra large condoms and a single carrot, fueling speculation. He warmly invited investigators into his home when they came a knockin'. He tried to open the package of condoms right in front of them with the observation that "For a lot of products that claim to have an easy open pack you almost need a light saber to get the fucking thing undone!" His conversation was mainly composed of wise ass cracks or Neo Platonist mishmash.

But wait! His live in woman was found to have a connection with Elisabetta De La Real – in a surprising discovery, diligent detectives learned that they had once worked together on a report about roller coaster accidents back in the days when Elisabetta led the statistical research squad at university. Now, there had to be something here – Elisabetta had been having an affair with the one who had experienced demise; Elisabetta knew the California man's girlfriend; the California man's DNA was in evidence at the murder scene. How were these dots to be connected? As we may all imagine the girlfriend, whose name was Rosaline Mercutio, was immediately asked to cooperate with the inquiry. It turned out that she was still obsessed with ride accidents, however, and was not available immediately because she was trying to interview victims who had been stranded 300 feet in the air for five hours on a ride at Knott's Berry Farm (they were given free t shirts as compensation for the ordeal). Rosaline Mercutio, like her friend Elisabetta De La Real, was visually unforgettable. She was a dead ringer for Mayo Methot. The lack of pep in her gait was instructive.

She had nothing to contribute.

What was her boyfriend's DNA doing at the scene of the crime?

When was the last time she had ever spoken to Elisabetta De La Real?

The dead man's face was everywhere – internet, TV, whatever print media still exists, all of it, for weeks and weeks. Someone named Popitone reported remembering encountering him once; he was working in a burger stand, sweating like a pig over a hot grill surrounded by incompetent co workers. Popitone asked "Do you guys have a restroom here?"

"No," the perished one had snarled, "we don't have a restroom. We just piss and shit in the corner over there."

Cheap Kenna Dipthong split Boston in a haze of little clarity. In the coming months she became embroiled in controversy over excerpts from a Wikipedia entry – something about the efficacy of identity politics:

"On July 28, 1991, Martínez pitched the thirteenth <u>perfect game</u> in baseball history, pitching for the <u>Montreal Expos</u> against the <u>Los Angeles Dodgers</u>. He was the first Latin American-born pitcher to pitch a perfect game"

In a stuffy room consumed with moonlight sits a spiritual policeman meditating. The case is years old now, unsolved, a file in the bottom of a cardboard box. This is a detective with psychological attunements – his own marriage, somehow, has survived tremendous blows inflicted upon it not only by himself but by his wife and children also. In spite of everything they had kept it going, like Willis Reed dramatically hobbling onto the court in game seven in 1970. This man had looked at corpses and corpses, had held the hands of innumerable weeping wives who were strangers to him, had seen the overawing bullet like eyes of killers and rapists more times than he would care to recount. He would be the first to tell you he could make no sense of human nature. Theories? Something for classrooms. Psychology? Please. An abstraction, a lounge conversation. He would be the first to tell you he could make no sense of human nature, though he had been on top of it, all over it, for most of his adult life. It had been right up in his face forever.

He sits in the quivering moonlight with the file in his lap, nourishing a thought that is not new but one that never fails to inspire awe, to inspire wonder – what is a human life, what indeed, indeed, but the unending accumulation of states of affairs and facts, the collection of questions that have no answers, the relentless pounding of experience fanning out in all directions.

Postmodern Deconstruction Madhouse (I)

Explorations of the one sentence short story.

1. He'd never wiped his ass with a coffee filter before.
2. All I can really do is try not to be perceived as a fucked homunculus right now.
3. She has a smile like an angel but a soul like nitroglycerin.
4. Braysha was tired of paying eleven dollars a throw for a bologna sandwich – God damn these people!
5. Every evening around six PM angry, hunchbacked women began to appear in the lobby.
6. All the babies we never made lay in scumbags in the bottom of the trash compactor.
7. She told me "I like Abstract Expressionism, foreign films, and Ornette Coleman" – I subtly gazed around the room, looking for an exit.
8. Here I am, sweating, huffing and puffing on the treadmill like a warthog, and the young lady next to me is just cruising along on hers like a fucking antelope.
9. West, the guitarist, had no personality whatsoever but, in addition to his massive aptitude with music, he was also demonstrating a distinctive flair for language; Stoy, the singer, made the crowds go wild but he could barely strum some elementary chords and couldn't put three words together; the record company insisted they

share the writing credit for every song, like Lennon/McCartney or Jagger/Richards, so there was some tension.

10. Donna has a parrot that can sing Beach Boy songs.
11. I've noticed that the blonde nun with the twisted radar eyes uses the non word "gayhood" when she means to say "homosexuality".
12. "I'm sick and tired of being lectured about ethics by people who buy bootleg DVDs!" I screamed at Uncle Sebastian.
13. Miranda asked Charles if he would like to accompany her to a lecture about how the nose picks up chemosignals from the sweat of the distressed.
14. A lover who tells you they don't care about money will lie to you about everything else as well.
15. Jasper's third daughter in law by his son Karl was an early pioneer in the farm to table movement in Karl's ribald suburban community.
16. He farted all the time, that oceanographer.
17. Veronica always ate curiously – she ate all the potatoes on her plate first, then the vegetables, then the fish – and she was not receptive to my questioning her about this bizarre practice.
18. Joan's boss laid it on the line to her – make do with huaraches or quit.
19. "You think it's been easy going through life with a name like Stookman Keetha?"
20. Police say that James Question, 27, of Manhattan killed his live in girlfriend, Nanette Dimo, 20, of Binghamton, by bashing her over the head with a tranquility fountain she had given him as a therapeutic gift to help him calm his nerves.
21. This douchebag Rory – he's the kind of guy who goes out jogging with his leashed dog, running in place while the mutt stops to pee.
22. The last thing Ed could remember was a tuba band playing the Pink Panther theme.
23. Marion had told me "His name is Hy, or Sy, or Ty, some short name like that that rhymes with eye" – so when he told me his name was Bo I began to grow concerned.
24. Nadreena made a comfortable living as an anthropomorphic tooth artist, drawing for dental offices, doing smiling individual teeth with faces, arms, legs, hands and feet, waving happily,

dancing, donning top hats and white gloves, brandishing miracle toothbrushes.

25. I enrolled in a "Past Life Regression" seminar in an attempt to score some loony babes.

26. I'd like a woman who looks good barefoot and can sing A Free Man in Paris all the way through.

27. The once fine lines of her body are now just inert clumps of angst.

28. This fucking dogface bitch is sitting in the waiting room in the doctor's office answering personal calls on her cell phone: "Hello Allan, this is Gail, you answered my ad on POF and I'm just getting back to you…"

29. We spend one seventh of our lives on Tuesdays.

30. "I have tea and biscuits and several board games, including my favorite, Husker Du."

31. Under the category of General Knowledge our team was asked what a citizen of Turkey is called and William answered "Turker".

32. I went to an ancient Italian barber for years and he always snipped the hair out of my nose but this Chinese girl won't do it.

33. She's always cutesy, like a bar called The Pour House, a hair salon called Shear Ecstasy or The Mane Event, or a dog groomer named Barkingham Palace.

34. I once took a course in defensive driving in which the instructor very gravely warned against having a bunch of stuffed animals lined up against the rear windshield of the vehicle – now I understand why.

35. I lust after her so hungrily I would believe I would eat her discarded toenail clippings.

36. Her benefactor is so old he calls cruise control in his car cruise-o-matic.

37. The old woman was so afflicted with osteoperosis, arthritis, and other ailments that she was unable to wipe her own ass while sitting on the toilet, so she would stand up and try to do it; often, midway through this action, she would be seized by such a sudden stab of pain that she would freeze in the pose, toilet paper in hand, and look like a discus thrower.

38. A few Mexican cunts were in there, whining.

39. A few Anglo cunts were in there, bitching.
40. Just when he thought he'd seen it all on Facebook with the They're Their There shitheads and the Your You're assholes, Bernard saw someone use "per light" for "polite".
41. In his memoir **As I Saw It** Dean Rusk writes that Harry Truman referred to Mao as "Mousey Dung".
42. Mysteriously, whenever she calls me she sounds as though she's in the kitchen of a Chinese restaurant – in the background I can hear harsh Cantonese, pots banging around, a steam pipe hissing.
43. The foe eloped with a shipwright.
44. Her planiped of choice resides in the Metuchen area.
45. Breaking boldly, forthrightly, with established traditions, Jack Baldi created new frameworks and perspectives hitherto unavailable to the hula hoop merchant.
46. A glazed youth in a kimono was standing around looking bored.
47. We, who turned to gazpacho in our loneliness, must remember that our nephews named their rock band Sex In Church before the cousins of doubt fell upon the snow bears.
48. The temporary security guard was caught humping a stanchion in the janitorial closet.
49. Her vagina needs an instrument cluster when I'm drunk; her pussy needs a switchboard when I woo her on the phone.
50. This fuckbird has spent half his life in court with Xpress Nap.
51. This fuckwagon believes he patented the Xpress Nap in the 1970s.
52. That little fuckchip over there won't use an Xpress Nap in Dunkin Donuts.
53. The Loins of the Apocalypse took the stage at nine PM.
54. She has the kind of face a caricaturist can draw perfectly with three lines and a swoosh.
55. I once worked in a large showroom on the harbor that had a huge front glass window; one morning as we were opening up the place we noticed that about thirty pigeons had flown into the glass at full speed and their smashed dead bodies were now all over the parking lot.
56. Johnson wondered why his teenage son was walking around the house trying to pick up common objects like pencils with his toes;

the explanation was that this was an exercise detailed in the Boy Scout Handbook, something about a merit badge.

57. If you have a great tattoo, why the hell am I complementing you – shouldn't I be complimenting the tattoo artist?
58. "I have a soft dick these days" was probably not what she wanted to hear, wouldn't you agree?
59. Before a camera a really sexy, good looking woman has a level of confidence most males will never get to in their entire lives.
60. Something like a human toe was growing out of the middle of my forehead (minus the nail).
61. If you had grown up in Philly in the 1970s her voice, from classic rock radio stations, would be emblazoned in your consciousness, therefore it was amazing to us when we heard it in its 2000s context.
62. Seven words that will always come back to haunt you: "I'll never need him (her) for anything anyway".
63. I love when a young woman walks by me on a warm summer morning and I can smell talcum powder on her – swoooooon!!!
64. We would discretely sit together in Starbucks at a small table for two; when she slipped me pieces of scone that her husband had baked for her my cock would get harder than it had ever previously gotten in my lifetime.
65. My contribution to the world of blues lyrics was "You know my feets is itchin'/Like Aleksandr Solzenhitsyn".
66. The film was made by Sam Pecky Pooh.
67. Bjorn Gonzalez had the meanest pimple you ever saw right in the center of his forehead, like a golf ball, red, juicy, with a rich, ripe green head, leading his colleagues to opine that he should wear a bandana across that forehead until such time as the insane zit had exploded.
68. The old queer was vomiting into the rice.
69. My mother's word for feces was "cackie".
70. My mother's term for defecating was "do a cacks".
71. My mother called flip flops "shower shoes".
72. I'm never eating here again – this fucking roast beef tastes like linoleum.

73. On many a morn her cunt had gibbous properties.

74. These kids today – their eyes glaze over when you talk to them about the Vietnam War, you might as well be telling them about the Peloponnesian War.

75. Polly Jupiter spent the summer laying around the pool, mixing vegetable juices in a blender and moaning fatalistically about fatalism.

76. My name is Peter; the Starbucks girl wrote "Eden" on my cup.

77. Bethany's entire life is an improvisation; as I talk to her this morning I see she's drinking instant coffee out of a takeout Chinese soup container.

78. Crossing Central Park in a cab at three AM, a bat flew into my taxi!

79. Lyle was so wasted at breakfast he asked the server for "Tuice, joast, beggs and acon."

80. If you want a true education in human nature just watch an unattractive person stare at an attractive one passing by.

81. When he opened his trench coat I thought, for a moment, that he might be a flasher – but no, the inside of the coat was lined with steaks that he had evidently shoplifted from a supermarket and he asked me "Hey buddy, wanna buy some steaks?"

82. I once went to a free outdoor jazz concert; at one point when the tenor man took a solo it seemed that his horn started broadcasting the radio signals from a passing police car.

83. If you insist that Shakespeare was a better poet than Maya Angelou you're a racist.

84. The gay film director annoyed the producers with too many shots of muscled beach boys throwing around a Frisbee.

85. McThune Baldi was fed up with subtlety and refinement, preferring to seize the initiative, acting on spontaneous impulse, challenging his boring coevals to drop trow and live, live!

86. O'Dylan Baldi was there as well, efficious and pontificating, holding up a hand like Arnolfini in Van Eyck.

87. "Medicine must develop alternatives to autopsies," Dr. Baldi stated, knowing full well that the elegant woman sitting across

the table from him at dinner wasn't listening to him at all but was, instead, daydreaming about French pension laws.

88. Puissant indeed she is, a curlicue bitch of perversion and disease.

89. Francis Attackman and Jacopo Sansovino hired a worthy, cheapened princess with a marked preference for blood to try and outflank Jack Baldi at the Chicago Mercantile Exchange.

90. It was raining on Election Day so we didn't go out to vote.

91. "We're going to Appleton, Wisconsin to pee on Joe McCarthy's grave," was the bewildering response.

92. Recent lesbian writing invites conjecture.

93. A whore she is, and intelligent – her whacky backhand compels rebuttal.

94. Few clandestine housekeepers such as Aponta ever shine my banister with a like degree of enthusiasm.

95. Lucinda Bishnobotto was making a pilgrimage to Lourdes with her several incapacitated children.

96. Savior Jesu, ayuda mi people!

97. The all important meeting – it could well decide the continued existence of the organization – was attended by the following executives: McThorren Hemagoose, Jr.; Octavius Thrisspintle III; Nervepun Stevewinter; Joe Brown; and Cavunkus Bluepost.

98. A sliced moan of grief came, softly, from behind the curtain.

Notes on MACBETH Posthumously Left Behind by an Undistinguished Scholar

Virginia Woolf – according to Jonathan Bate in *The Genius of Shakespeare* – opined as such: "…the truest account of reading Shakespeare would be not to write a book with a beginning, middle, and end; but to collect notes without trying to make them consistent." This is very sage advice, and I will try to be faithful to the spirit of it here.

*

Every so often in the news we see a report emanating from a third world nation – a captain, perhaps, or a colonel, sunglasses on, pistol on his hip, has stormed the palace with his junta and led a coup. We should understand – his great capacity for poetry, eloquence, and introspection not withstanding, Macbeth is exactly this kind of thug.

*

The amount of literature in existence about *Macbeth* is unmanageable for any one individual. I'm a novice. I've done very little reading in the slatternly intermezzo we call Theory; one reason for this is what seems to me to be Brian Vickers' utter demolition of it in *Appropriating Shakespeare*.

Most of my reading on the play has been in the type of criticism that I'll call the High Lofty which, in my judgment, is just as dangerous for studying Shakespeare as Theory is. Essentially Bardolatry on steroids, some of the notable practicioners have been Van Doren, Goddard, Hazlitt, Bloom, Bradley, Nuttall, etc.

The grandmaster of Shakespeare criticism is, in my inexpert view, Spurgeon. I will return to her case for regarding Macbeth as a mean, cruel, and petty man way out of his depth a little bit later on.

*

My overall view is that, like it or not, in this day and age the most profitable way to get a handle on Shakespeare is to view the many different presentations of a given play that are available on film in conjunction with as much primary and secondary reading as one cares to do. Of course, we know that down through the ages numerous critics have taken the position that Shakespeare is primarily for reading, not for performance. Granted, many of these critics mainly had the theater in mind, but we can comfortably assume that they would hold the same opinion of the cinema. (As an example of this sort of belief, Goddard writes somewhat contemptuously of "some obliterating actress" playing Rosalind in *As You Like It* and why the "imaginative man" always prefers to read the play rather than see it. Lord!)

This point of view is most unfortunate. I say this because one can be the most profound, insightful reader in the history of the Milky Way galaxy and still not be able to intellectualize and visualize with more profit than one can get from a viewing a few different cinematic interpretations of a play and comparing them against each other and against Shakespeare's words.

Here are two examples, both from offerings of the Scottish play, of the enormous power of the cinema in articulating Shakespeare:

1) In Casson's 1978 film featuring the Royal Shakespeare Company, the early scenes show one of the three witches broken out in an intense feverish sweat, barely able to walk or speak. She is quite noticeably in this condition; the other two are not. Much later on – most graphically during the "Tomorrow and tomorrow and tomorrow" sequence – McKellen is shown in the same state of heated physical fervor. The visual implication is unmistakable: the same possessing spirit that gripped her body is now gripping

his. Whether or not we feel this to be a legitimate interpretation of Shakespeare's writing is beside the point, which is that it would be extremely unlikely for this impression to be gotten solely from reading.

2) In Jack Gold's film for the BBC series in the early 1980s the sky, in the scene in which Duncan, Banquo and others arrive at Inverness, is lit a brilliant and intense orange behind them. The gate of the castle stands opened, and the bars of it, sharpened at the ends like swords or spikes, are filmed in the foreground in such a way that they appear to be coming down right on the heads of Banquo and Duncan. This visual evocation of danger and betrayal anthropomorphizes the castle in a way I don't think reading alone ever could.

*

Yet, obviously, reading the plays allows us to compare them with each other, and thus get a sense of Shakespeare as a whole, in a way that viewing films cannot. Nuttall makes an important point in both *A New Mimesis* and *Shakespeare the Thinker* - that Shakespeare often recycles but never merely repeats himself.

As an example, take some lines from *Macbeth* that could just as easily have been in *Othello* – "There's no art to find the mind's construction in the face" and "False face must hide what the false heart doth know". Someone with a full command of all the plays, I'm sure, could fill many many pages with examples of such criss crossing. I'm a novice, similar to Colin Wilson with *The Outsider*.

*

What is *Macbeth* about? A small sample of comments from The Big Lofty will give us some ideas of what some have thought.

Goddard actually claims that the knocking scene is "a poetical effect beyond the capacity of the stage" and that no actor can possibly properly capture the intended effect of the line "This is the door" that Macbeth utters to Macduff after the murder of Duncan. This is all to be tied in with an alleged voice from "the bottom of the universe".

In his introduction to a Pelican edition of the play Harbage writes that Shakespeare at his sharpest can push up against the boundaries of what is expressible in words and that "Some of the speeches seem to express the agony of all mankind." In an introduction to a Signet edition Barnet writes that "When one sees or reads *Macbeth* one cannot help feeling that one is experiencing a re-creation of what man is, in the present, even in the timeless." Bloom makes the astounding statement that "Shakespeare rather dreadfully sees to it that *we are* Macbeth, our identity with him is involuntary but inescapable." And so forth.

All these are outrageous, unprovable sorts of claims that are characteristic of The Grand Lofty. Elaborate metaphysical speculation might make our spirits soar for a while, but in my estimation we do well to be perhaps a bit more grounded. What do the characters in the play actually do? What is the genesis of their activity? What they do in large measure is **deliver and receive messages, news bulletins and reports which, in the main, recipients do not question the veracity of and which, in the main, contain true and accurate information.** Indeed, the words "report" and "news" and their synonyms appear quite often in the play.

Below I present twenty examples from the drama to support my observation and comment briefly.

ONE

Act 1, Scene 2 - Here the bloody man delivers a report – and Duncan actually says "He can report" – about Macbeth's bravery and courage.

A word about this – Duncan seems to be excessively trusting. Perhaps this is why he is habitually betrayed by people like Cawdor and Macbeth. It seems a trifle odd to me that, for instance, he is relying on the contingency of a chance, accidental meeting with a wounded soldier for information about how his own army is performing. Wouldn't the king have an extensive network of spies and scouts? (As Macbeth himself is shown to have once he becomes king.)

TWO

Act 1, Scene 2 – Ross arrives to report of Macbeth's bravery versus Norway. Again, Duncan appears to be relying on complete happenstance for this important information. He doesn't even recognize Ross, one of his own thanes!

THREE

Act 1, Scene 3 – Here the three witches report to each other. Largely irrelevant.

FOUR

Act 1, Scene 4 – Here Malcolm brings news to Duncan of Cawdor's execution. The scene is important because it stresses Duncan's naïve consciousness. He mentions his "absolute trust" in Cawdor – he is about to place the same in Macbeth, with a worse result.

FIVE

Act 1, Scene 5 – Macbeth's letter to Lady Macbeth fills her in on the prophecies of the witches and their subsequent coming true. It's important to note that the witches' predictions early on are given full credence while, further on, the importance of their later ones is perhaps not fully appreciated by Macbeth.

SIX

Act 1, Scene 5 – The servant brings Lady Macbeth the news that Duncan will visit that night. Notice that in this brief conversation both "tidings" and "news" appear, thus strengthening the theme.

SEVEN

Act 1, Scene 7 - "How now! What news?"

EIGHT

Act 2, Scene 2 – Macbeth reports to Lady Macbeth the killing of Duncan.

NINE

Act 3, Scene 1 – Macbeth reveals (to the audience) through his dialogue with the hired murderers that he has reported news of Banquo's wrongdoings against the murderers to them, the murderers. This is the one place where we might wonder if the news report in question is true or not. It may not be – Banquo does not appear to have been the type for malicious foul play.

TEN

Act 3, Scene 4 – The Murderer brings the news of Banquo's killing and Fleance's escape to Macbeth.

ELEVEN

Act 3, Scene 6 – The unnamed LORD reports to Lennox that Malcolm and Macduff are in England seeking the aid of Edward.

TWELVE

Act 4, Scene 1 – The apparitions deliver predictions which we may consider news by this point in the play, though I acknowledge this characterization might be questioned.

THIRTEEN

Act 4, Scene 1 – Lennox reports to Macbeth that Macduff has fled to England.

FOURTEEN

Act 4, Scene 2 - The messenger arrives to advise Lady Macduff to flee.

FIFTEEN

Act 4, Scene 3 – Ross brings Macduff the dreadful news.

SIXTEEN

Act 5, Scene 2 – Caithness provides Mentieth will military intelligence.

SEVENTEEN

Act 5, Scene 3 – "Bring me no more reports."

EIGHTEEN

Act 5, Scene 5 - Seyton gives the news of Lady Macbeth's death.

NINETEEN

Act 5, Scene 5 – The messenger reports that Birnam Wood is moving.

TWENTY

Act 5, Scene 8 – Macduff gives the news that he is not of woman born!

Thusly, twenty instances of the motif. This is evidently a world in which delivered messages count for much – or, to be more accurate, at least a play in which they do. It would be well beyond the scope of my knowledge or expertise about medieval Scotland to state categorically that "This society functioned in large measure on the backs of messengers" although such a statement is probably a good guess.

It is also a likely good guess that much more could be learned about this play from an intensive study of the available literature on the psychology of dictators rather than wanton High Romantic Bardolatry about "unseen forces that shape our lives" or New Historicist wish fulfillment about the tenets of Elizabethan society or, gulp, Parisian effluvia. I grant you that very few people who are interested in imaginative literature (let's cling stubbornly to the term) either as a career or a hobby are going to want to put in the time and effort required to slough through much technical work on said psychology, but I would not hesitate to bet that a careful study of the life, say, of Pol Pot or Saddam Hussein would reveal quite a few dispositions to behavior similar to those of Macbeth. (Goddard, to his credit, recognizes the applicability of parts of the play to the behavior of certain twentieth century dictators. So does Mary McCarthy in her essay. Rupert Goold sets his film, about which I will have much to say, upon this very idea as a basic operating principle.) If there is any kind of universalism to be found in literature it is in comparative research such as this.

Another important topic to be given attention in the overall study of *Macbeth* should be, I venture, the psychology of ambition. George H.W. Bush was once asked why he wanted to be President of the United States. His answer was "For the honor of it all." This seems to me to be exactly the kind of ambition the Macbeths exhibit, a kind of directionless, ambiguous desire for glory – holding a position just for the sake of holding it, with no higher or more dignified purpose -which is fine, given that there are probably very few of us who could articulate the meaningful goals behind our ambitions at a moment's notice. And again, I understand that there are most likely not a lot of people who work in the humanities who are going to be inclined to do reading of this sort (I mean technical research in clinical psychology), and we probably don't have enough information on the Macbeths' background, their lives before the play, to definitively state the motivation for their ambition to be king and queen, but it's fairly clear to me that this desire is entirely selfish and comparatively shallow and superficial, not unlike the desire of Kim Kardashian or Paris Hilton to be celebrities. Scream if you want, but show me the differences based on the available literature about the research.

*

In *The Mystery of Macbeth* Amneus, despite some rather tortured arguments about various other subjects, make the golden observation that when Shakespeare hits upon a narrative problem he often simply ignores it and hopes the audience doesn't catch it, or else he resorts to poetry. In *Macbeth* there are two giant problems of this nature. In his film Roman Polanski actually comes up with a logical, though perhaps unintentional, solution to one of these.

The problem is as follows. Early in the play Macbeth and Banquo, on their way to Forres, stumble upon the witches on the blasted heath. The witches ambush them, speak for a short while, and then vanish into the air. Later, Macbeth wishes to consult with them a second time. How does he know where to find them? I may be wrong, and I apologize if I am, but as far as I can see Shakespeare doesn't tell us how Macbeth knows where they are. The fact that he does find them is a glaring example of plot contrivance. Polanski gets around this by having Macbeth and Banquo stumble upon the witches' lair on the trek to Forres – they actually see where the witches "live". (Amusingly, one of the witches is brushing another's hair as Macbeth and Banquo approach.) Now, it is necessary for Polanski to show us the lair due to the little twist he throws in in the last seconds of his film, but it solves the earlier problem nonetheless – Macbeth is given a landmark with which to work.

Here's a second problem of the narrative: Macbeth and Lady Macbeth plot to kill Duncan so that Macbeth may ascend to throne. However, Macbeth is not properly the next in line – Malcolm is. Yet, in the course of their planning, the Macbeths make no provisions whatsoever for this inconvenience. They simply plow forward as though Macbeth is the rightful successor to Duncan. Of course, Malcolm flees and so the point as a matter of practicality is made moot, but this is just a happy coincidence. How might the play be different if, upon hearing of his father's death, Malcolm had said "Well, let's start making the arrangements for my coronation right after dad's funeral"?

*

Act 1, Scene 1, of course establishes the eerie tone of the play. As happens in almost all celluloid Shakespeare, Polanski cuts the original text to ribbons in order to suit his purposes.

"I come, Graymalkin." "Paddock calls." "Anon." To a diehard purist the cutting of these lines may represent a cardinal sin; to someone acquainted with, but not totally obsessed by, the play it may or may not even be noticed; and to someone counting this film as their first exposure to *Macbeth* it obviously won't matter very much at all. Polanski not only cuts the dialogue - he rearranges it and moves it around in spots as well. Here, the first words the witches speak in this scene are "Fair is foul..."

etc., which in the scene as Shakespeare wrote it are the last words they say. It's not an effective choice. The difference between having a character ask the question "When shall we three meet again?" as the leadoff speech on the one hand and having three characters chant a slogan in unison on the other is actually monumental. In the first case we might immediately think things like, Oh, they meet regularly. Oh, their preferred meeting conditions are thunder, lightning and rain and not pleasant beach days that are eighty degrees and sunny. Oh, I wonder why they meet anyway, and so on. Hearing them chant a song doesn't produce this kind of reaction. Shakespeare's original order is much more effective.

That said, the opening shots of a beach locale changing colors – first red, then brownish-gray, then blue, with seagulls singing overhead, establish the undeniable visual beauty of the film that Polanksi and his cinematographer Gil Taylor maintain throughout. The three weird ones walk into the frame from the left, pushing a little cart along in the sand. They stop, kneel, dig in the sand, and bury a severed human hand with a dagger positioned in it, as well as a noose, in the cool wet earth. They quickly make a little grave out of this, pouring potions over it and spitting. The few lines of dialogue are spoken by only two; the youngest, most "attractive" one doesn't speak at all (she is the one who later flashes her female parts at Macbeth and Banquo after the first prophecies are delivered). Here they speak calmly, conversationally, almost casually, something they do not do in the other three films I am going to discuss here. The wheels of their cart squeak as they go off down the shoreline, and then the screen goes blank as the credits begin to roll against the background noise of the battle where Macbeth unseams Macdonwald.

It isn't easy for me to assess whether or not this clip establishes the mood Shakespeare had in mind for this opening scene. (Also, we must never forget the personal circumstances under which Polanski was making this film.)

In *Shakespeare* Van Doren wrote "Darkness prevails because the witches, whom Banquo calls its instruments, have willed to produce it. But Macbeth is its instrument too, as well as its victim. And the weird sisters no less than he are instruments of an evil that employs them both and has roots running further into darkness than the mind can guess." Employs them for what purpose? To kill Duncan? Is it that evil employs the sisters to kill Duncan and they subcontract the work out to Macbeth? Or is just that evil desires to produce random general mayhem with no specific targets? What is this evil, anyway? What kind of ontological status does it have? What kind of existent is it?

A final observation on this section – Polanski is a strong filmmaker with a very recognizable style, much like Kubrick or Antonioni. Therefore a serious student is going to want to refer not only to Shakespeare but also to earlier films of this director such as *Knife in the Water* and *Rosemary's Baby* for reference.

*

Which brings up the question – should one view films of Shakespeare's works as a film critic, or as a Shakespearean? If there be anyone at all in the cosmos with any interest in what I have to say here, they would likely be one of three things - a student of literature, a film buff, or a Shakespeare Phreak. Depending upon one's orientation, the attitude and approach will vastly differ. A film buff would be perfectly willing to consider Polanski's film of *Macbeth* on the same plane as an aesthetically brilliant but intellectually empty movie such as *The Thomas Crown Affair*; on the same plane as one of Chabrol's psychologically acute and weird thrillers; and on the same plane as a Hollywood screwball comedy from the 1930s, and every other kind of film we care to name; a hardcore Shakespeare enthusiast would not be quite so willing. In fact, to such a one to compare all these as equals would probably be heresy.

(If I may briefly insert this as well – there are almost always live theater productions of the play going on somewhere. Even as I write this Kenneth Branagh's acclaimed staging at the Armory has just ended and a Sydney Theater Company production featuring an avant-garde design by Alice Babidge is opening. I reluctantly omit theater from this discussion simply because it's hard to consult or refer to after the fact of the live performance is over.)

*

Casson's 1978 film of the Royal Shakespeare Company's interpretation is done in a theater-in-the-round; the two opening shots establish and define the boundaries of the playing space first with an overhead shot and then with a ground level shot as the cast members walk onto the stage and sit in a circle. The camera then pans the faces of the actors in a circular arc. A church organ plays the identical theme it will play later at Macbeth's coronation. Although many of Shakespeare's plays engage in reflexivity, Macbeth as he wrote it does not (except maybe for the porter scene and 'equivocation'), therefore reflexivity as it exists here is Casson's insertion. It's a little bit, though not quite exactly, like the opening of *The Taming of the Shrew.*

Casson's staging of the scene is deeply interesting. The three witches emerge from the circle and group together. One seems to be limping, and she sweats with intense fever (this is the same kind of feverish look McKellen is swathed in from the time of the rituals they perform on him in Act 4, Scene 1, on till the end of the production. – the implication is that the witches put this same spell that is making her sweat into him with their rites). The witches tremble and chant unintelligibly. While this is going on we see Macduff (who at this point is unknown to us as Macduff) leading Duncan to an area where he begins to kneel and pray so that we simultaneously see the witches buzzing and humming and Duncan praying. Duncan kneels and prays with his sons; Macduff, however, doesn't – he stands, with his arms folded, watching. Duncan wears a huge cross around his neck, so we might assume he is engaging in Christian prayer. Thus we are shown Duncan's Christianity against the witches' paganism, clashing like two cymbals. This point is further stressed in later scenes with rituals and dolls.

Two of the witches speak calmly; the feverish one wails loudly, almost appearing to be in pain. Thunder and lightning ripple.

Recapping – the master strokes here are the fever, an introduction to the establishment of Macduff's personality and character (which is greatly built upon shortly), and the referencing of Christianity.

*

Jack Gold's interpretation, done for the BBC Shakespeare series in the 1980s, is in some ways very traditional and conventional but quite bold and original in others; the opening scene of the play, with the witches, falls into the first category. It is complete vanilla, total decaf. (Although we must acknowledge that Gold makes inventive use of the witches in later scenes.) The boring credit sequence does, however, do one thing, and that is establish the powerful soundtrack. All four films we examine here make use of commentative music, but in this film it is truly noteworthy.

Two further points – of the four filmmakers I will discuss here, Gold was the most skillful with cinematic techniques at the time he made his *Macbeth*; and Barnet's comments on this film in the Signet edition are overly dismissive and borderline disgraceful.

*

Rupert Goold's 2009 film is even more "movie like" than Polanki's in that it immediately establishes a strong ***mise-en-scene*** in the *Cahiers du Cinema* sense of the term. Like Polanski, Goold cuts Shakespeare's dialogue and moves it around and, again like Polanski but in a more extreme way, he does so right off the bat, in the first scene, so that the "What bloody man is that?" scene comes first. Here it's done for the sake of modernity – the witches appear as nurses in a MASH unit (later they appear as kitchen help in Inverness, participating in the preparation of meals), handling modern medical equipment, but they are anything but nurserly. In fact, they seem quite menacing.

The film opens not with them but with a bloody hand opening and closing, then a quick cut to what looks like some stock war footage of canons and soldiers running in fields. Next, in the same grainy black and white, we see Macbeth and Banquo in the woods, making their way back from the battle. The three witches are dressed as nuns and, as we said, working as nurses upon the captain. Their aprons are splattered with blood.

The body of the bloody captain convulses on the stretcher. The narrow tunnel passageway, a minute before buzzing with people and activity, becomes eerily empty. The captain's heartbeat stops; he dies. The first sister asks angrily when they should meet again, roaring the words. When the third sister says "There to meet with…" she looks directly into the camera with a sinister glare, which is only appropriate since in the next moment she pulls the dead sergeant's heart out of his chest with her bare hand.

Each viewer has to decide for themselves to what degree they can accept this experimentalism. My own inclination is to welcome this sort of risk taking, even if it causes small absurdities. (An example – "Upon the heath", yet, they meet with him not on any heath but in an empty banquet room.) (Additionally, in this case flipping the order of the first two scenes around seems to matter in a way it does not in, for example, Kenneth Branagh's 1988 production of *Twelfth Night* for the Thames Shakespeare Collection.)

Finally, the strategy lends an interesting element to the sisters in the sense that it has them participating in dual realms, both in the real world action of the play (as nurses) and in their traditional role as supernatural predators.

*

In my opinion, Shakespeare's comedies are much stronger than his tragedies. The writing in the latter seem very forced to me as compared to the comedies, which flow quite a bit more smoothly and naturally and display a much deeper understanding of people. The Deep Lofty takes a different view – if you happen to be reading a book on Shakespeare and the chapter or essay on *Much Ado About Nothing* is five pages and the one on *Macbeth* is twenty five...

*

The number of debates and arguments about the three witches is infinite, and many of them down through the centuries have been of an essentially trivial nature; it does seem to be a no brainer that the Hecate scenes are by Middleton, or at least by someone other than Shakespeare.

Hazlitt wrote of the difference between what he took to be Lady Macbeth's eagerness and anticipation and the witches, who are "...who are equally instrumental in urging Macbeth to his fate for the mere love of mischief, and from a disinterested delight in deformity and cruelty. They are hags of mischief, obscene panders to iniquity, malicious from their impotence of enjoyment, enamoured of destruction, because they are themselves unreal, abortive half-existences – who become sublime from their exemption from all human sympathies and contempt for all human affairs, as Lady Macbeth does from the force of her passion!" We can let this quasi hysterical passage stand alone and speak for itself without a lot of comment, but I find it hard to refrain from remarking on the classification of Lady Macbeth as sublime, and when we get to the appropriate scenes I would like to revisit this as well as A.C.Bradley's discussion of the character of the lady.

Lastly I beg your indulgence to briefly observe that some critics, for example Henry Cunningham (editor of the 1912 edition of the Arden Shakespeare) thought this scene to be spurious on the grounds that it contributes nothing to the drama; others, for example L.C. Knights, opined that this scene establishes a major theme of the play, which in his view is "the reversal of values".

*

Having the advantage of big Hollywood money at his disposal Polanski is able to set up grand outdoor shots – this scene (Act I, Scene 2) evidently takes place on the same coastline or beach where the three witches have just met and where, after the credits stop rolling, we have just seen a small and intensely brutal snippet of the battle – hair raising and not for the squeamish. Thusly is made the interesting suggestion, with all its attendant implications, that the witches have previously visited the scene of the battle.

Shakespeare's poetry is butchered again here, but a lot of information is given visually. For one thing Duncan, Malcolm, and Donalbain are on horseback, and so is the captain of "What bloody man is that?" fame. In fact, accompanied by another rider, he approaches Duncan on his own power, as his own jockey. Duncan is clearly older than everybody else but he is not the elderly, genteel sort at all.

As the man with the bloodied face speaks we would do well to focus on Malcolm and Donalbain. While the story of Macbeth's great bravery unfolds Malcolm is clearly upset and worried, dismayed to hear that Macbeth has done so well. In contrast Donalbain laughs and celebrates along with everybody else (we will investigate the meaning of this laughter presently). It is of special importance to notice Donalbain here in light of the non Shakespearean hook about him that Polanski throws in at the very end of the film, and to note Malcolm for the following reason: his fretting over Macbeth's ascension shows that he is completely ignorant of his father's intention to shortly name him the Prince of Cumberland. Each of us can decide for ourselves what this means about the family's dynamics and about Duncan's communication skills. It may mean absolutely nothing at all, but I don't think this is a plausible interpretation of Polanski's interpretation of Shakespeare's intent.

Another unique feature here is that Ross, when Duncan and his sons thunder up to him on their mounts, is shown to have brought the treasonous, captured Thane of Cawdor along. The thane is restrained on his back, shirtless, on a very painful looking device. Duncan looks down at him with a glare of absolute loathing and hatred, and picks his thane's medallion off his neck, by the chain, with his sword – casually flipping it to Ross to deliver to Macbeth. This Duncan is a harsh, rough, unforgiving, brutal man, and this leads to a point I want to make about the laughter in this scene.

At the end of the film when Macbeth's head is put on a spike and paraded around, everyone laughs – they crack up at this as though it were entertainment provided by the court jester. This is the same type of laughter that erupts when, in this scene, the bloodied soldier (in Shakespeare's stage direction he is called a captain but Malcolm calls him a sergeant) speaks "Unseamed him from the nave to the chops" and the same kind of jeering group laughter we see later in the witches' underground cave. Men who laugh at these kinds of things – a severed head, an unseaming, prophecies of great doom – can only be living in a savage, dog eat dog kind of world. Too, of Macbeth, the line "Well he deserves that name" is not spoken directly but is instead spoken from afar, by someone off camera, kind of thrown into the conversation from left field.

*

Whereas in Polanksi's film Duncan is on horseback, on the move, at the scene of his army's victory, Casson's film paints quite a different picture. Here the king is elderly, stationary, immobile, barely able to move under his own power, presumably at camp or perhaps even in his castle. He's seen with his sons, Lennox, and Macduff (who is not identified and who, as far as I am able to tell, is not named as being present in this scene in any printed version of this play that I can find). Yet repeated viewings show that one of Casson's main intentions in this scene is to introduce Macduff and his bearing.

Old Duncan, a large crucifix around his neck, is praying, head bowed, as are his sons and Lennox. Macduff, however, doesn't pray but stands over the others with his arms folded, observing, as if waiting to be convinced of something. The bloodied soldier clacks up, and Duncan says only "What bloody man is that?" "He can report...etc" is cut. Casson, like Polanksi, edits the original, though perhaps not to an identical degree.

As the soldier begins to fall to the ground on "My gashes cry for help..." Macduff, anticipating, rushes forward to try and catch him – the second time in just a few minutes that we have seen him give literal physical support (he earlier assisted Duncan when the actors broke out of the circular theater in the round setting). This all serves to immediately establish him as a strong, silent type, perhaps foreshadowing "I have no words – my voice is in my sword."

After some overly theatrical screaming the bloodied messenger is led away to surgeons and Ross and Angus enter.

It occurs to me, seeing Macduff resume his place behind Duncan as Ross says "From Fife, great king" that Macduff is Thane of Fife – wouldn't he be present at a battle taking place in his hometown? In any case, here, as Ross speaks of the turning of Cawdor, a look of hurt, pain, and sorrow crosses Duncan's face – nothing like the hatred and loathing that showed up on the face of Polanksi's Duncan. What a contrast in countenance!

On "...the victory fell on us" those that were formerly in prayer return to it, while Macduff closes his eyes in thanks and visibly heaves a sigh of relief; and Ross presents a check for ten thousand from the Norweyan lord, a prop not used in any of the other three films we discuss here – a nice touch.

According to Casson's vision, Duncan speaks the lines about making Macbeth the new Thane of Cawdor to Malcolm instead of to Ross, whereupon Malcolm, stunned and overwhelmed, stammers and hesitates. Ross then touches Malcolm on the arm gently and says, "I'll see it done." To my knowledge this interpretation is unique.

I'll comment on a minor irritation here. I understand this is theater tradition, and I also understand that in this case it may be due to budgetary restrictions; in live theater this would possibly go completely unnoticed but on film it is very obvious – the actors who play a witch, Donalbain, the bloody captain, and Ross all play other parts in the film as well, all too recognizably so. This amounts to whacking the window pane of the suspension of disbelief with a sledgehammer.

*

For the most part Jack Gold's film adheres to a very straightforward, realist, traditional, conventional approach. It's a "fourth wall" type of philosophy with one or two small exceptions. In this scene, as far as I am able to determine, not a single word from the original is cut. Unlike the first two films, we don't get a lot of silent, unarticulated angst on Malcolm's part. In fact he is portrayed as being open, honest, good hearted, earnest and loyal – not an anxiety ridden calculator.

In this scene three things dominate – the set and scenery, the bloody soldier, and Ross. In other words, the basics. And what basics indeed they are.

In a countryside lit by a firey red sky and a huge red ball of a sun, on what looks to be parched ground, with smoke and dust everywhere in the air, Duncan, his sons, Macduff, and other nobles come upon the bloodied captain, who is doubled over in pain, on his knees. Macduff is present but, unlike in Casson's film, he here is a virtual mannequin and quite irrelevant. Gold has the camera start on the group and then backtrack, shooting from behind the captain, not quite over his shoulder. After recognizing the captain and identifying him to the others, Malcolm moves forward to stand by him while he relays his knowledge of the broil. Malcolm's earnestness is indicated by the warm and hearty way he says, "Hail, brave friend."

This bleeding valiant man gazes around in a shocked daze, as if he cannot believe the king is really there, and he shakes himself free from Malcolm's steadying, reassuring grasp as if to say Don't touch me, I'm all right. Yet he holds his side as he speaks and when, after making an unseaming gesture with an air sword, he grimaces mightily in pain, clutching his side.

As he speaks he looks down, and to the side, in the kind of eye movement that contemporary schools of psychology such as Neuro Linguistic Programming would claim is significant - he is looking into the past in his mind's eye.. Thusly, the depth of preparation here on the part of both the actor and the director is really impressive.

And when Duncan asks if Macbeth and Banquo were dismayed by the second attack he looks at the king with what is almost contempt before answering. Unlike Polanski's and Casson's films, where the bloody man simply has some blood on his face, here there is a true attempt to realistically portray a wound, to portray suffering. As the captain is being led away on "Go, get him surgeons" Ross and Angus are already stepping into the frame from the rear.

This is perhaps noteworthy, I don't know – when Ross and Angus kneel before Duncan Angus is a step or two behind Ross, and he stays there during Ross' reports (this is repeated shortly when the two of them seek out Macbeth and Banquo). I assume this is meant to signal that Angus is of a slightly lower rank. The set design of small hills smoking with the residue of battle is deeply impressive – this is moviemaking that understands the collaborative nature of presenting Shakespeare to people who might not be all that familiar with his works.

Ross speaks calmly, composedly, conversationally (as is not the case in any of the other films). The outstanding characteristic of his report to Duncan is that he seems both a little surprised and a little hesitant to hear that Macbeth is being made Thane of Cawdor, which perhaps might lead us to conclude he is a little wary of Macbeth and might just perceive his (Macbeth's) behavior to be reckless and crazy rather than brave.

*

Since, as mentioned, Goold plays with the order of the scenes, the bloody captain's speech/report is essentially the first impression of the play a novice viewer gets. He opens with traditional Hollywood style establishing shots – in this case, what appears to be stock World War Two footage gotten from a library or newsreels. This is followed by quick cuts to Macbeth and Banquo making their way through the woods to reach what I'll call Tunnelworld, which is where most of the play takes place (although the larger geographical location would seem to be a mid twentieth century European dictatorship).

Dramatic music is played over the shots of the feet of the three witches pushing the stretcher that holds the bloody captain. It dawns on us that Tunnelworld is being shelled, bombed, is still under attack, as Duncan and his entourage come upon the bloody man. This is unique. In the other films, indeed I would venture to say in most presentations of the work, the fighting is finished, done with and over by this time.

The bloody captain is on the stretcher with his chest ripped open; he chokes out the speech as a last defiant shield against death, but it doesn't work – he dies. He talks to Duncan as Malcolm and Donalbain flank him on either side, supporting him, their gazes moving from the captain to their father. When he speaks of the hare and the lion he guffaws; when he speaks of the unseaming both Malcolm and Donalbain smile broadly. It almost looks as if the three witches kill him, unplug his machine (this film features much twentieth century technology) although I can't be sure about this.

As Duncan and his sons make their way through the maze of Tunnelworld, Ross runs up to them, out of breath. This is a geeky, meek Ross, a little bit of a nerd. On the news of Cawdor's betrayal Duncan gives a look somewhere between the Christian heartbreak of Casson's Duncan and the murderous vengeance of Polanski's. The reference to the funds Macbeth's victorious army has received from Norway is deleted; Malcolm emits an enthusiastic whoop on "The victory fell on us." One of the witches walks right by Duncan on "…noble Macbeth hath won." This insertion of the witches into the body of the action gives the film a very eerie, supernatural edge.

*

A brief recap: in the four films we see Duncan depicted in four very different ways – on horseback, vigorous and ornery, at the scene of the concluded battle; humbly and meekly praying; walking with his entourage near the scene of the battle; and in a mobile army hospital that is being bombed by the enemy.

*

Postmodern Deconstruction Madhouse (II)

Self indulgent metafiction with notes.

Monica (one of my roommates) has all her course work completed for her PhD in film studies. **(0)** It'sjust a matter of the dissertation now. Her scholarship concerns Sam Peckinpah. She's watched *Bring Me the Head of Alfredo Garcia* more than a hundred times. This created the peripheral consequence of her writing an analysis of Warren Oates' performance as Dance in *Ninety Two in the Shade*.

You may or may not know that the republic is leaden with the insanity of intellectuals, mainly in its hallowed halls of learning. **(1)**

Unwell in her body, Monica pukes incessantly. I know why - she desires anorexia. She sticks her fingers down her throat after every meal, on purpose. I often see her lurched over the toilet, heaving, butt crack exposed by the drop of her jeans. She has white girl droop, that I can say with confidence. And she has no tramp stamp - no tattoo at the base of her spine - either. Her face has its own laws. Her cheeks are hollow one day and puffy the next. Often, her hair hangs across her eyes like mutant spaghetti. In quiet moments she reflects with feeling about Preparation H Medicated Wipes (not the liquid).

"You know those little labels on pieces of fruit in the supermarket?"
"Yes."
"What are they? What are they for?"
"So the checkout girls know what code to type into the scanner."

"They're the reason I throw up. I eat them. I don't peel them off the fruit. They must disturb my stomach."

That was the last thing I heard Monica say on that humid, unbearable summer morning. Well, next to last. She was throwing her backpack over her shoulder, off to do more research, and, looking out the window, observed, "Oh, here comes Petite Conical Breasts. You can chat him up, he's always a lot of fun." And off she flew.

I observed the young man who was nicknamed Petite Conical Breasts as he came sauntering down the block, whistling, carrying, as he often did, a rolled up poster under his arm, his other hand in his jeans pocket. Anybody who knew him - who knew the town, really - knew what the poster was. It was wall art from Burger King, where he worked as a manager. His apartment was said to have Burger King posters all over the walls, ones that said GIVE THE GIFT OF BEEF or GET SWEET ON THESE or EITHER WAY, YOU'LL BE CHILLIN'.

He saw me looking at him through the porch window and gave a friendly wave. **(2) (2a)** The nickname came to stick to him in this manner: at a poker game one night, he and a bunch of other young souses got into a discussion of the most memorable features of their most memorable experiences with females up to that point in their young lives. Most of the guys gave very standard, run of the mill, quotidian analyses of the circumstances involved within their memories. He crossed his arms across his chest, right hand gripping left shoulder and vice versa, tilted his head to one side, closed his eyes, sighed dreamily, and cooed, "Oh, she had the most beautiful petite conical breasts." This surprising description caused quite a hoot, and thus the sobriquet. His real name was Nogs Berga.

A cab screeched up in front of the house, the top floor of which I shared with Monica and two others, and out bounced one of those two others, Chookie **(3)**. Honey tanned skin, white teeth, machine gun conversation, that was Chookie. She was from a rich Argentine family and had a constant, unending string of new lovers of either sex. It was profoundly unclear what she was doing enrolled as a student at a university. Notably, she had gainful employment as a phone sex girl. In this position she made more money than some doctors and lawyers. There was no door to her room, just a curtain, and in my movements about the house I frequently heard her on a call making transparently insincere gasps of ecstasy and moans of an orgasmic nature that led me to wonder, Who is on the other end of the line paying $6.49 a minute for this? Once I heard Chookie say into the phone, "You have to understand, this is something that I usually do while I'm doing the dishes or my nails with a cuticle scissor, but you're dynamite! You got me so wet it's dripping down my leg!" Whenever Chookie was upset with Monica she would patrol the apartment for dust bunnies, gleefully curling them up into round pellets between her thumb and forefinger, and flick them at her adversary like a spitball. It was widely speculated that it was because of her status as a paragon of world exotica that Chookie was among the first crew of table servers at the Bed Supperclub in Bangkok who paraded around mostly naked with the menu tattooed on their bare skin; she did this over a summer vacation. *****

Chookie bounded out of the cab and into her room without a word, and Petite Conical Breasts continued on his way down the street. I had to pick up my stuff at the dry cleaners, so off I went. It was a short three block walk to the main drag of town. On the way I encountered Professor Lucien Cartha at his car. The hood was up and he was working on the engine with various tools. His face, hands and shirt were a grease stained mess. Cartha, of the Political Science department, was a bitter man indeed. He had once had experience in practical politics, actually running for office in Utah, of which he was not a native. There were accusations of carpetbagging which were corroborated with drama when, in a debate with an opponent, trying to describe the citizens of Utah, he said something that sounded like "Utons" (rhymes with "futons"). Realizing this wasn't right, he tried to cover with "I mean Utahians," and the audience hooted. Agog, he said "I mean Utah people," and that was essentially the end of the campaign though he struggled on another few months. He even got about thirty seconds on **Hannity & Colmes,** if I recall.

"Hey Lou," I nodded as I went by. (4)

"Fucking piece of shit!" he screamed at the car engine, bent over it, wrench in hand, ignoring me.

The humidity was oppressive, and the interior of the dry cleaners was even worse, with no AC. A humungous power fan rocketed hot air into your face as you came in. The place was owned by two ancient Greek immigrants who were there six days a week, twelve hours a day and who, I was certain, had to be millionaires many times over from this business. I say this even though the place looked like hell with the walls peeling and crumbling. If you read a book like Stanley and Danko's *The Millionaire Next Door* you would see, immediately, what I mean. **(5)** But the place was like a time warp. Even though everything, including the owners, was old and fading it had always been old and fading in the same yellow way for the several years I had been a customer. The place looked exactly the same now as it had always had, as though at a certain point in the aging process the aging process itself had come to a halt, frozen in time.

Absurdly, every time I picked up my cleaning I got a reminder of one of my exes. Why? Because I still used her name on the tickets the old lady wrote out for me. This ex had a simple monosyllabic American name whereas mine was foreign, complicated and long. This woman at the counter would be struggling there with trying to write my own name forever if I used it with her, so I just kept using that of my ex all down through the years. Even that, the simple name of my ex, was a struggle for her. She would lean her body over the counter, the pen held in midair, waiting for me to spell it so she could write it on the ticket. A weekly occurence, for years. Sometimes I would hesitate a minute before spelling just to watch her standing there, holding the pen in her veiny hand, looking down at the ticket, waiting to write the name. The fan rumbled in our faces like an airplane propeller. I began the walk home with my shirt drenched in perspiration, dropped off my cleaning, and walked over to the so-called Internet Cafe to have a coffee and cool out a little with my friend The Augustinian/The McGee. **(6)**

Seated at one of the few computers in the so-called Internet Cafe was a young fellow, an alternative rock looking kind of guy, talking in hushed, urgent tones on a cell phone. On the computer screen before him was an advertisement banner showing a cartoon of Britney Spears in a leather and chains bikini, twirling an infant over her head like a baton, with the caption IS BRITNEY A BAD MOM? VOTE! ********

The Augustinian/The McGee was at our usual table in the corner. I was late. I signaled to the young waitress for a coffee and joined my friend. Today The Augustinian/The McGee was made up to be The McGee. Let me explain. Years ago when he got his PhD in English and literature he had specialized in the ***Confessions*** of St. Augustine, which still obsessed him to a major degree, but in the intervening years he had also become increasingly interested, both in an academic sense and in a life sense, with the literary implications of detective fiction, and the Travis McGee stories by John D. MacDonald were his favorites from that genre. According to what his overall mood and intuition of the current state of his karma were at any given time he carried himself and dressed like either St. Augustine or like Travis McGee. Today, obviously, he had been in the tanning salon in order to create the whole Travis McGee/Florida image. He wore jeans, moccasins with no socks, a cotton shirt that wasn't ironed and unbuttoned halfway down his chest, a gold medallion around his neck designed to contrast with the deep tan of his skin. He and I cultivated a deep friendship partly because he wanted to some day write a major academic paper comparing Augustine's friendship with Alyppius as chronicled in the *Confessions* with that of Travis McGee and the economist Meyer in the McGee novels; a real life friendship was therefore a most utilitarian help in this regard. I think the essay *On Friendship* by Cicero, a favorite of Augustine's, was a factor here as well.

Being amateur film enthusiasts, peridocially The Augustinian/The McGee and I would meet to pretend we were screenwriters in Hollywood pitching scripts to a producer. We alternated in the roles of screenwriter and producer; today, as per an arrangement made on the phone prior to the in person meeting, we would pitch one new idea each. After, we would drink coffee and go bowling, trying to pick up younger women (in their twenties or thirties) for the remainder of the afternoon and evening.

"Bro," I said, extending my hand. He stood, clasped it, pulled me to him, we bumped shoulders, we sat.

"What's happening Peter?"

"Nothing, what's up with you? Thanks honey," I said to the young waitress. Then I remembered a line I had heard in a Date Younger Women seminar, so I tried it on her. "Before you go, can I ask you something really quick?"

"All right," she said, holding a large white napkin under the silver coffee pot she had in the other hand. "Quick. It's getting busy." The coffee shop was kind of ablaze with chat and human clutter. She was about twenty and probably just starting to break a few of the many hundreds of hearts she would crush in the course of her lifetime.

The Augustinian/The McGee waited with as much anticipation as the girl herself.

I said, "Tell me...would you date a guy who still slept with his teddy bear?"

She arched her eyebrows - it was the moment when the recognition of her female power, and its applicability to the scenario, kicked in. She couldn't hold back the laughter. "Why? Do you still have a teddy bear?"

I shrugged. "Not me, necessarily. Just as a general overall principle - would you?"

She thought. "I don't know. Is he cute?"

The McGee offered, "Just in the abstract."

Suddenly her recollection meter turned on and she smile broadly, even sexually. "You mean maybe like one of those custom made Vermont Teddy Bears?"

"Hey, hey! Where's my bagel?" someone called, and with a quick wink our waitress scurried off to attend to that.

"What do you think? Am I going anywhere?"

"She winked. Maybe."

"You think she's too young?"

"No. No way." He struck the pose of an orator and quoted:

"The billions upon billions of lives which have come and gone, and that small fraction now walking the world, came of this life-pulse, and to deny it dignity would be to diminish the blood and need and purpose of the race, make us all bawdy clowns, thrusting and bumping away in a ludicrous heat, shamed by our own instinct." (7)

"Well," I opined as she came back with my coffee, placed it in front of me, and immediately ran off to serve her waiting minions without a further word to us, "that's certainly authoritative enough for me." I noticed out of the corner of my eye that she was flirting with a group of students closer to her age as I put a little cream in my coffee.

We sat like two grandmasters of chess, across the table from each other. A coin toss had determined that I should go first with my log line; the idea was to encapsulate the essence of an entire movie into one paragraph, as few sentences as possible, to make the "producer" want to see the entire script. I began:

"A man starts an affair with a wild young thing. His wife, who always suspected this of him, hires a detective to confirm it. Upon receiving the confirmation she makes a plan to murder herself and the lover, deciding that removing both from her husband's life will be her greatest revenge. Knowing that the lover works as an instructor in a driving school, she disguises herself, acquires false identification, and enrolls as a student in the school. She eventually plans to crash the car on the freeway during a lesson, with herself and her husband's lover in it, maybe drive it off a cliff to ensure certain death. The husband unravels it all at the last minute and has to race against time to save them." I had been hunching forward as I told the story; finished, I leaned back in the chair.

The McGee let out a low whistle. "Pretty good Peter. I can see the roles - Antonio Banderas, Demi Moore...but who for the wild young mistress?"

"Her." I motioned with my chin at our waitress, who had swished by at that very moment with her ass packed so finely into jeans. We laughed heartily, then it was time for The McGee to go.

"A man brings his brown bag lunch to work every day and stores it in the refrigerator in the break room. One day he opens his sandwich to find that the meat has been removed from it. Someone took the meat, leaving the bread, lettuce and tomato but removing the meat from the sandwich." He beamed at me proudly. He was normally much more parsimonious with displays of emotion; while he smiled at me he made a sudden grimace that was quite normal for him due to an old injury that had roots in the plantar. He grimaced perhaps three hundred times a day.

I waited for more but he just continued smiling at me stupidly. "That's it?"

"What do you mean, that's it?"

"Where's the conflict? The protagonist and the antagonist? The drama? You know, the Lajos Egri?"

"No no, the idea is to create interest to hear more, not to tell a complete story."

"That sucks. That's the worst fucking log line ever! Nobody would buy that."

As he launched into a spirited defense I found my mind wandering, not really paying attention, coasting off into a sort of life review - a grand excursion of memory.

I've fallen extraordinarily hard three different times in life - once in politics, once in the music business (the blues, specifically), and once in the world of art. At sixty it's time to reflect. At forty I had come to understand a couple of things. First, that the consequences of our ignorance often become the content of our sorrow; second, that my higher ground consisted of four things: literature, chess, the blues, and pussy.

In these reflections I start with a comparatively recent set of events, then move backwards. At sixty, sharing a house with a group of college kids as roommates (Monica, Chookie, and Javiac) doesn't really make me proud but it's where I've landed. I have an eternal safety net which has always bailed me out - the automobile business. I'm one of the world's foremost experts on leasing cars to Americans, and I have been for eternity.

My son and his friends have chosen a name for their punk rock group - **Piss Creation**. What do you think about that? Would you believe that this has given rise to some protests within our community? Should I be worried? He's thirteen. (He says **The Suck Off Party Wenches** was also a strong contender.)

Last year I had a sort of semi-serious relationship with a spunky woman of forty. Here's how our breakup came about: aimlessly surfing You Tube, I discovered to my great amazement that she'd released a "booty shaker" video of herself on the site; in two months it pulled in 476,348 hits. I recognized everything - her living room, the furniture, the view from her window, her plants, her butt, her snakeskin thong, the tattoo of the caduceus at the base of her spine. I immediately grew bitter and jealous because she surely never shook it for me the way she was doing in that video! My immediate reaction was to angrily confront her about it, but then I realized I would have to explain why I happened to be on You Tube surfing for booty shakers and that was something I didn't really want to do. As a consequence I made up some contrived issue that I pulled out of the air and forced it all the way to its logical conclusion, which was that we should go our separate ways. I told this story in my cock support group to much acclaim.

Please permit me a segue here. When Douglas Ivester was the CEO of Coca Cola in the late 1990s he came up with the following idea for outdoor Coke machines: somehow they would be hooked up to a thermometer which would automatically raise the price of a Coke as the temperature got hotter. There's a reason why this never became reality, of course - the backlash would be merciless. People would eventually grow to hate the Coca Cola corporation. In a conversation about this someone once suggested to me that a person such as Dale Carnegie would have advocated the opposite idea, which is to say that as the mercury climbed higher the machine should *lower* the price. Surely that would rake in millions. My initial reaction to this second proposition was yes, of course it would, people would love Coke for this benevolent practice. But then it occurred to me that that hasn't become reality either. Why hasn't it? **(8)**

I humbly ask that you hold this anecdote off to the side for a moment; we shall come back to it. I believe it contains an important principle.

> Recently, for perhaps the twentieth time since I got my first AOL account in 1994, I traveled a long distance to meet someone whom I had previously only known online and through a few phone calls. Our online relationship was extraordinary, and I was expecting that our meeting in person would be the same, but when we finally did hook up and hang out for a little while the meeting was so strange that I'm sure each of us thought the other was insane. We met at what is, to judge from the press the place gets, the hippest restaurant in Seattle, How To Cook A Wolf. It's most certainly neither my place nor my intention to practice restaurant criticism here, but I will say that this establishment is quite an experience. I wondered how it would do in New York, if it would survive, and found myself unable to come to a decisive opinion in this regard. (My internet friend, a Seattle local, gave an emphatic thumbs down.) **(9)**

Here's another anecdote, something of a personal one. Be patient with me. This was at a Barnett Newman exhibit - at the Philadelphia Museum of Art, if I'm not mistaken. One of the works was this gigantic, immense, absurdly large canvas painted yellow. That was it, the whole thing, all there was. It was called either Yellow Painting or Yellow Canvas, I don't remember which exactly. People were mystified. One man indignantly remarked, "Christ, what a ripoff! They call this art?! My kid could do this! I want my money back!" So that was one point of view. I walked around a bit, checked out some other things, came back, observed a scholarly looking woman in professorial glasses rubbing her chin in thought and saying to a couple of friends, "Hmmm...I think the point of this is supposed to be something like...well, like, how would you explain what the color yellow is to a blind person, someone blind from birth? You can't. It has to be seen. It would be like trying to explain the smell of coffee beans to someone who has never smelled them. How can you do it? So that's what I think this is about - the wonder of sheer, raw perception, of taking perception for granted, you know? Like what Wittgenstein said: **What can be shown, cannot be said.** Right? You can't open your mouth and make the color yellow come out - all you can do is point to it." So that was a second point of view.

You see a pattern emerging - it has to do with perspective, with differences of perspective. I had one perspective, the woman I met in Seattle, my internet friend, she had another perspective. The perspectives were not compatible.

You know how it is - like Montale forever writing poems about the unattainable woman, the woman who's always and forever just beyond his grasp. Is that correct? Was that Montale? **(10)**

I say to you: she typed me two or three messages that drove me out of mind. I mean, I melted. But to her they were just confident, assertive remarks that she didn't think twice about.

I say to you: in the course of one afternoon we once typed over four hundred messages to each other on My Space.

By way of example, let me try this another way, via another woman. I fear my communication skills might not be up to the task. It's always so hard. We'll call her Myla, this woman from long ago and far away. I used to witness her magnificence in the gym. Sometimes she came in with her man, sometimes alone. If they did come in together they would split apart quickly and work out for an hour or so on opposite ends of the gym, doing different things. The only way you would know they were a couple is if you saw them come or go.

Her pulchritude: what can I say? How can I express it in a way that the great romantic poets already haven't? All I can tell you is that she had lines on her body like a classical statue and I would watch in silent torture while she did some bicep curls. You know how it is in a gym - you know a person is checking you out but you don't come out and acknowledge it - yet something secret in your demeanor lets them know that you know. For many, many weeks I would bop up and down like a madman on the elliptical machines and watch her exercise while pretending not to. But these things, these vibrations, they rise and encircle - a couple of times, mostly in mirrors, I saw her looking at me.

Myla did both weights and cardio with equal fervor, equal drive, and when she did cardio she was always reading a book, usually a big fat hardback. The first time I caught her looking at me she was framed under the red neon sign that shouted CARDIO. And so a curiosity began to develop. When she came in alone she would briefly catch eyes with me, for a flickering second, a quick and passing smile forming at the corners of her mouth, and nod ever so slightly. Yet when she came in with her man she avoided even this minor bit of acknowledgement, acting as if I were invisible or not there at all. I just puttered along in this condition. My imagination had me licking individual beads of sweat off her shoulder blades many, many a time while I drove home from the gym after seeing her. I'm sure you get the picture.

In Augustine's **Confessions** there's an episode where his father notices for the first time, in the public baths, that Augustine's grown into manhood. The thought that this triggers in him is the rather selfish **good, grandchildren soon.** Do we today view our legacies any differently than Patricius did? I can't decide - can you? What I can tell you without hesitation is that Myla often reduced me to a steaming pail of lust, much like the young Augustine, and I thought of his youthful news often.

And so one day I bounced on the elliptical machine like a lunatic, with my eyes closed as was my wont, no one on either machine on either side of me. I pumped my legs with gusto and meditated on the status of the universe. You know, Berlinski vs. Dawkins, shit like this. It's always hard.**(11)**

Suddenly my intuition kicked in and I knew someone was on the machine on my right; not only that, I knew it was Myla. I mean I *knew.* Her scent was in the air, exciting me, enlivening me, her overwhelming presence was capturing my wussbag self. I opened my eyes with a peripheral shift. Myla was starting to get going, her fat book in her hands, unopened. She was staring in disgust at the television. Now, I knew Myla never looked at the televisions that hung above the exercise equipment. She always read. In this particular instance the book she had in her hands was ***Danger and Survival: Choices About the Bomb in the First Fifty Years*** by McGeorge Bundy. It was an enormous book; maybe she carried such big books en lieu of weights while she worked on her cardiovascular processes? This possibility was considered.

The television facing us was on a channel showing an episode of ***Girls Gone Wild.*** I immediately caught the implied scenario - she thought I'd been watching ***Girls Gone Wild***! Lord! I felt as though she'd caught me masturbating in the closet - I wanted the earth to just swallow me whole. The truth was, it had been on the television before I got there and I didn't even pay attention. Myla smiled that little smile at me and started reading while she pedaled; I went to the front desk, got the remote, and changed the channel to a nondescript nature program. Within moments this new show featured a male hippotamus mounting a female from the back, thrusting, near a river. Even though there was nothing even remotely resembling human passion and it was a purely mechanical act, I imagine that my face was scarlet red. Myla looked at me, however, and now the smile was openly wicked. I was reduced to stammering. She was back into her book in seconds. I shut my eyes and pedaled, and when I opened them she was gone. I felt like an idiot. Whatever 'shot' with her had been dropped in my lap, I'd blown it. "Unrequited" isn't quite the proper word, but hereafter I began to feel the kind of romantic longing feelings that have kept the poets in business throughout the centuries. I won't attempt to be poetic (and I, admirer of Isaiah Berlin's essays on romanticism!) but the pangs of emptiness in the center of my body began to hurt. I was wallowing. (And somewhere in here the woman I had been dating steady for six weeks began to complain.)

This melacholy went on for some months. I could never escape the feeling that she wanted to talk, wanted to get to know each other, wanted to break free, but that she felt trapped by her circumstances. Sometimes her eyes - jewels from the bottom of the ocean - told me these things. There was nothing we could do.

Some time later, early one Sunday morning in the supermarket, I wheeled my cart around a turn and BANGED! into another one coming around the bend from the opposite way. Guess who it was? And she was in her gym attire...how many times had I dreamed of this woman in these clothes? Hundreds, thousands. You know how it is when a person's face really makes an impression on you, their features begin to appear to you like the broad strokes created by a master caricaturist, so that their visual essence becomes imprnted on your consciousness. It gets harder and harder.

"Hey!" I said, affecting an easy laugh. She laughed too and giggled, "Hey you! Steer better next time!"

"What you got there?" I asked, picking a pack of frozen vegetables out of her cart and examining it. "I'm sure you eat healthy."

After a brief discussion of fruits and vegetables she had a question. "Hey, is the gym closed today or what? I was there and the front door was locked, it looks deserted."

"It opens at eight," I said.

Her brow furrowed." I thought they were open twenty four hours."

"Not on the weekends. They close at eleven."

A light bulb lit brightly, suddenly, in her eyes and mind. "Ahhhhh, that's it."

I smiled. "You were there early?" I was wondering if her man was with her, maybe out of view in an aisle poking among the fruits or meats.

She smiled; she tossed her hair, and my palpitating heart with it, over her shoulder. My cock started to hurt, thinking about the knots of muscle in her thighs and calves. "I was."

A quick check of the time demonstrated that the gym would be open in a few minutes. I ventured, "So...I'll see you on the bike, after shopping? Gotta run." I was trying to use some variations of some principles from Robert Greene's works, though it's unclear to me now if Greene's books were even out then. It may be that I intuited the vailidity of the ideas before I came across them in coherent book form. **(12)**

"You definitely will," she said with mischief, turning her cart past me and wheeling it over to the whole grains. "I was a little out of control last night with the pasta." And she pinched an inch, or tried to because there wasn't one, on her love handle area, thus guaranteeing that I would masturbate with her in mind for the next three weeks. ***Sigh.***

I never saw Myla again - I mean literally not ever, never. In a certain sense, I had fucked her so many times in my mind that it really didn't matter but, of course, in another way it did.

I'm not doing very well here in my attempts to make you feel the crater of emptiness. I'm not doing well with it by talking about my Seattle friend nor about the lost and beloved Myla. Therefore I am going to undertake the task of telling about my adventures in the art world, and that'll be coming up next.

NOTES

I play John Fowles at this point and comment on the novel a bit. Remember, Joyce said he was able to pack in so much that it would keep the professors going for a thousand years (I'm paraphrasing) - but I'm not Joyce and fear that this work will fall, as Hume said of his *Treatise On Human Nature,* deadborn from the press, as it is. It isn't clear to me just how helpful such notes are - recall Hal Hartley's remark "I don't look for explanations for human behavior because there aren't any."

(0) There was a point here at which I flirted with having the narrator Peter and his roomie Monica discuss an essay about the J horror film *Shutter,* possibly writing a scene in which Monica, having been selected by her film school professors to judge an undergraduate essay contest, asks Peter for help with the task, or perhaps Peter himself would try his hand at film criticism and have the expert Monica read his work. The film *Alpha Dog* was given excessive consideration here as well. I

never really worked out the details because I killed the idea. I left it on the cutting room floor of the story but there's nothing to prevent us from preserving it in the notes:

Shutter

Of course, even before entering the theater, I knew that going to check out the latest J-horror film **Shutter** would involve putting up with fifty 10-14 year olds shrieking out fake screams of terror, making snide comments at the screen loud enough for everybody in the theater to hear, and texting and talking on their cell phones throughout the picture. This is just an extension of school, or the mall, or a friend's basement. The idea that the cinema could be a place housing art as important as any museum doesn't occur to kids this age. Of course, it doesn't occur to most adults either, and in combing through about twenty online reviews of this film I see it doesn't even occur to many people who are paid to write about the movies for a living. Too bad; if most films are given a chance they certainly repay the effort. **Shutter** definitely does.

The film begins with the wedding reception of a young American fashion photographer, Ben (Joshua Jackson) and Jane (Rachel Taylor). The shallowness of Ben's personality is telegraphed immediately, the very first time he speaks - he tells the wedding guests, "Thanks for coming, let's all eat some cake." His character flaws are the linchpin on which the whole picture hangs, so this is important. Immediately after the wedding and consummation the couple whisks off to Japan, where Ben has a gig, for a combination of work and honeymoon. While driving on an isolated country road at night Jane hits a young woman, but no trace of her can be found afterwards, even by police search teams. In due course a strange white streak of light starts showing up in Ben's photographs. His assistant suggests this looks like 'spirit photography' in which the spirits of the dead show up in photos, usually looking for revenge. As it happens, the assistant's ex boyfriend runs a well known Japanese magazine devoted exclusively to this subject. When Ben and Jane visit him he says the spirits that show up in these photos often do so because of 'unrequited love', which will eventually turn out to be the case here. The mysterious girl whom they hit on the road is Megumi, a translator with whom Ben had an affair on an earlier assignment in Japan. He just wanted a fling, but she was looking for much more, and when he dumped her she started stalking him. Ben's friends Bruno and Adam - American expatriates who live in Japan - got involved. It all ended very tragically, and now her ghost is back for revenge.

Although this is allegedly a 'horror' film, that is a superficial classification. There really isn't a single truly scary moment in the entire picture. My personal opinion is that it is no longer possible for any film - not just this one - to scare audiences in the way that, say, **Psycho** could when it was a new type of cinematic experience. So in order to have our cinematic hunger gratified we have to look for other things.

I've always felt that the existing body of films from the past can provide us with a way to pariticipate actively in a new film, and that is either through obvious direct visual quoting or through a scene that at least awakens a memory in us of a prior film, even if this is not the director's actual intention. One example in **Shutter** : the characters see images in photographs of things that were not physically present in the time and place of the photograph. This immediately conjures up the scenes in **The Omen** where the exact same phenomenon prophetically occurred. And, of course, the truth and/or falsity of what a camera can capture has been a cinematic peroccupation since **Blow Up.** And an image that Kubrick played with in **The Shining** - that of a woman who appears to be sexy and beautiful from the front but who is revealed in actuality to be a decomposing corpse when we see her from the back - shows up here as well. And these are just three examples that I caught in just one viewing, in a theater with sixty screaming kids around me throwing popcorn. And I don't think it really matters very much if the director (Masayuki Ochiai) has the specific intention of quoting or referring in this manner, or not. If he does, fine; if he doesn't, it speaks to the power of the images in their own right and for their own sake. And it jostles the viewer's imagination into making connections for itself.

We hate to dabble in cliches, but as directed by Ochiai and photographed by Katsumi Yanagishima the poetry of the images is breathtaking. Aerial views of both New York and Tokyo are outstanding (and the natural beauty of Mount Fuji too). The visual style is very cool, very steely and detached, very ice blue in tone. I mentioned ***Blow Up*** earlier, and I think the way the hipness of 1960s London was portrayed there is a very defiinite influence on the way a sort of international, boundaryless hipness of today - personified by the sensational Maya Hazen in female mode and by the near brilliant James Kyson Lee in the masculine example - is done here. Ochiai, like Michael Mann, has the gift of being able to speak volumes of exposition without dialogue. As an example, Jane's jealous nature is communicated twice by facial expressions, reactions she makes to how Japanese women approach Ben, with crystal clear clarity without a single word being spoken.This film is really about things like, How much should you know about your spouse's background? What is the nature of stalking? Of taking justice into your own hands? And finally it's about the blending of cultures into a true kind of internationalism. Again, a lot of this is visual. The Tokyo skyline could just as easily be the skyline of an American city. The young Japanese professionals throughout all speak English and dress like Americans, just as Ben and his friends move easily and fluently through the Japanese language and customs. Not overtly political at all, but definitely functioning in a manner as to indicate we're all going to be moving deeper and deeper into Global Village mode as the twenty first century advances.***Shutter*** is pretty capable moviemaking. Don't believe the (negative) hype.

Alpha Dog

Here's a movie about spoiled, rich Southern California white kids whose lives mainly consist of drug abuse, meaningless sex, and posturing violence. Are you still awake? Actually, the fact that the plot, the characters, and the setting have all been done umpteen times before shouldn't be an automatic disqualification by any means as long as some of the other elements of filmmaking are strong enough to make up for the shortfall. Here's the problem though, and it's a pretty insurmountable one - everyone's a bad guy. Dramatic tension only comes across when we have really strong feelings for the good guys and equally strong ones for the bad guys. You know, protagonist(s) and antagonist(s). Here all we have is one dirtbag versus another. With a couple of small exceptions every character in the film is either despicable or stupid.

Johnny Truelove (Emil Hirsch) is a marijuana dealer with a stable of low life thugs and followers including the doomed Elvis (Shawn Hatosy), Frankie (Justin Timberlake), and TKO (Fernando Vargas). Jake Mazursky (Ben Foster), an out of control drug addict, can't come up with the money he owes Truelove. When he tries to talk to Truelove about some more time and a pay plan, Truelove attacks him - huge mistake. Jake's a black belt in the martial arts, and after he pulverizes Truelove in the fight he proceeds to humiliate him in front of everybody by calling him too chicken to use the gun Truelove pulls on him, which turns out to be true.

Meanwhile Jake's younger brother Zack (Anton Yelchin) has a fight with his parents when they fight a reefer bong in his bedroom; after he runs out of the house we see him wandering through a park. Guess who just happens to be cruising by in their van? Right, Truelove and his cronies. Seeing the opportunity, they grab the kid and plan to hold him for ransom for the money Jake owes. We're supposed to believe that they're so stupid, ignorant, and young that they don't realize kidnapping is considered to be one of the most serious of crimes - they treat the whole thing like a kid's game. And this is one of the main points the the picture is trying to make, though you have to look really hard to see it - these are all just wannabe adults, children pretending to be grownups. The film goes to some length to indict the parents, particularly Truelove's father (Bruce Willis) and Mazursky's mother (Sharon Stone, in a good performance that's almost wasted by the way her character is changed in the last scene in which she appears) - both of whom are seen in journalistic footage that is supposedly taken way after the main events of the film transpire. Frankie's father is a pothead who invites his son to join a menage consisting of himself and two girls half his age.

The film is loaded with tattoos, drugs, rap music, gorgeous SoCal mansions with swimming pools, etc. The only two characters with any straight and narrow sense of right and wrong are Frankie's girlfriend, Susan (Dominique Swain - who by the way has the best biceps in the picture in spite of all the males who aspire to that title!) and the burnout druggie Keith (Chris Marquette), who refuses to be complicit in the story's appalling conclusion. Chuck Pacheco as Chucky Mota is good too in a brief role that seems to capture the entire essence of Southern California in about six speaking lines.

Alpha Dog requires patience and a willingness to grant the benefit of the doubt. There are a lot of loose ends (for example after a while Jake, who dominates the story up to a certain point, simply disappears - he simply falls off the screen and is never seen again); director Nick Cassavetes tries to be artsy at times (the image of an evil laughing clown is snuck in under the radar in back to back scenes), to his credit. If you have an open mind you may like this film, but it's going to take some work.

(1) "Monica" is the name of the mother of St. Augustine. The signifcance of this comes a little later in the chapter. I believe I once read in Marshall Fine's biography of Sam Peckinpah that, at the end of his life, the director was so far gone that he was betting the resurrection of his career on *Bring Me The Head Of Alfredo Garcia*. The film version of Thomas McGuane's hyper-literate novel starred Warren Oates as the antagonist Dance. One of the great problems of my style is that I can easily fall into a *Tripmaster Monkey* sort of trap where it seems that every other sentence contains a direct or indirect reference to a work of cinema or literature. I have no decent solution as to how to resolve this.

(2) Burger King posters are much more interesting than those of other fast food chains; the ability to write persuasively, to hook the reader (the consumer) is not a subject that the *literati* takes much interest in, but I list the following sources as an introductory guideline:

James B. Twitchell, *Twenty Ads That Shook The World*

Juliann Sivulka, *Soap, Sex, and Cigarettes: A Cultural History of American Advertising*

Jackson Lears, *Fables of Abundance: A Cultural History of Advertising in America*

Steven Fox, *The Mirror Makers: A History of American Advertising & Its Creators*

I believe too that hard to find works by the best copywriters of all time, such as Rosser Reeves and David Ogilvy, or a study of the great ad campaigns of all time (such as those that Doyle Dane Bernbach did for Volkswagen in the 1960s, or some of Leo Burnett's work), give a particular sort of insight into human nature that the arts cannot.

(2a) Chain restaurants and fast food joints are virtual laboratories for the study of all aspects of human culture and behavior. As I write this I'm glancing at a story in *The Wall Street Journal* about adults, accompanying their children at various points of Chuck E. Cheese's around the nation, getting into violent fist fights and brawls, (Story: Tuesday, 12/9/2008).

3) "Chookie McCall" is a character in *The Deep Blue Good-By* and other Travis McGee novels by John D. Macdonald. We'll discuss this shortly.

***** See the *New York Daily News,* Sunday Now section, Sunday, December 28th, 2008.

(4) So much, if not all, of modern politics is perception. In point of fact all 'debate' in contemporary American politics is a continuation of the competing theories of democracy of two Harvard professors, John Rawls in *A Theory of Justice* and Robert Nozick in *Anarchy, State and Utopia*. But such loftiness of purpose is wholly absent in American political discourse. It's just easier to catch your opponent in an affair or to dig up something of a dubious nature that they may have said thirty years ago that has little bearing on anything today.

(5) Many high falutin' literary types seek to skewer any sort of endeavor that can be classified as self help, or self improvement. Without getting too much into that sort of debate, the effect that a book such as *The Millionaire Next Door* can have on anyone who reads it, meditates on its chief points, and takes it seriously is bound to be life changing.

(6) Regarding the unusual naming of this character, I got this inspiration from the amazing novel *Logic* by the amazing novelist Olympia Vernon. I discuss this in some detail in my article on this novel in *The Bohemian Aesthetic*. Of course there are also excellent general discussions of names and naming in literature, for example in *The Art of Fiction* by David Lodge.

**** On my view Britney Spears is the kind of cultural phenom that must be taken seriously. I read, with eager attention, the sort of minute by minute breakdown of the MTV documentary about her, *Britney For The Record,* offered in the December 12, 2008 issue of *Entertainment Weekly.* Kevin Federline is also a great subject for socio-political inquiry and probably a potential dartboard face in Postfeminist Theory seminars. As an aside I mention that the cover figure of that same issue of that same magazine, Jennifer Aniston, appeared nude or semi-nude on a few magazine covers around that same time - clearly to taunt Brad Pitt. It was opined on a "Culture Warrior" segment of *The O'Reilly Factor* that Aniston looked great and was an inspiration to forty year old babes across the land that they can still be sexy and deliver the knee weakening visual joyride (not by O'Reilly but by his panelists).

There was never any question in my mind that I would be using Augustine's *Confessions* as one of the literary obsessions of this character, and I hope some of the appreciative text in the novel shows why. It is simply one of the most amazing works of literature in all civilization and, besides, I wanted something from antiquity. However the second selection was not so easy. I considered The Baldwin, The Bellow, The Updike (or The Updikean), The Archer (after Ross Macdonald's detective Lew Archer), and The Shaw (Irwin, not George Bernard). Simply from an aesthetic, that is to say a visual, perspective I think The Augustinian/The McGee looks best, and I also happen to feel it sounds the best on the tongue as well, the most harmonic. Compare:

The Augustinian/The Baldwin
The Augustinian/The Bellow
The Augustinian/The Updikean
The Augustinian/The Archer
The Augustinian/The Shaw

or, alternatively, with the names reversed:

The Baldwin/The Augustinian
The Bellow/The Augustinian
The Updikean/The The Augustinian
The Archer/The Augustinian
The Shaw/The Augustinian

My articles on Baldwin and Bellow at *The Bohemian Aesthetic* hopefully convey the depth of admiration I have for these authors, although in the present work I probably would have used *Tell Me How Long The Train's Been Gone* rather than *Another Country* and *The Adventures of Augie March* instead of *The Dean's*

December as representative works. (In passing, I opine that Einhorn in *Augie March* was the first pre-Internet character in literature who had an Internet Lifestyle consciousness.)

Of Updike I have never written in print, but permit me in the overall course of these notes an observation or two, starting with something plucked at random out of *Memories of the Ford Administration,* an overlooked and awesome novel. As always, Updike's sex scenes are exceptionally and descriptively graphic, a little bit too forced, too finessed, but in any case they aren't for me the driving force behind the greatness of this novel. That lies instead in the way the narrator, Alf, talks about the husband of his lover, Brent Mueller. Mueller is a representative of the "New Thinking" in academia, in American intellectual life - in other words, he's well versed in French Theory (Lacan, Derrida, Barthes, Foucault, etc.) while all the other mummified professors in the department at Wayward College are still stuck in the ancient age of Liberal Humanism as exemplified by Leavis. Indeed, the whole novel seems to be about the creation of history; we gape in awe (at least I do!) at the way Updike has Alf report in rich, lavish prose his detailed constructions of episodes in the life of James Buchanan (complete with sources and references!) while simultaneously having Brent dismiss this all as just so much noise. Look:... " - a certain Brent Mueller, who while landlocked at some Midwestern teachers' college had deconstructed Chaucer right down to the ground, and also left Langland with hardly a leg to stand on. Brent, a pleasant enough, rapid-speaking fellow with the clammy white skin of the library-bound and the stiff beige hair of a shaving brush, explained to me that all history consists simply of texts: there is no Platonically ideal history apart from texts, and texts are inevitably indefinite, self-contradictory, and doomedto a final aporia. So why not *my* text, added to all the others?

The brilliance speaks for itself, and I have nothing to add.

An excellent contemporary novel that sort of mirrors the structure of *Memories of the Ford Administration* is *The Melancholy Fate of Captain Lewis* by Michael Pritchett, well worth some time and effort.

I'll briefly make the following comment, however, about the word *gemutlicht* that appears in the novel, only because it also appears in an earlier Updike novel, *A Month of Sundays*. I didn't have to look it up because it's discussed in an audio vocabulary program from Nightingale Conant that I've owned for years, *Winning with Words* by William A. Koehnline. Let me share with you the biographical information on Mr. Koehnline contained on the program's cover: "He is not only a lifelong student of words, but has specific, practical experience in most of the fields which compromise the seven basic cassettes featured in *Winning with Words*. For example, in the field os art, Dr. Koehnline has a keen appreciation for not only literature, but drama, dance, opera and sculpture as well. He is currently a member of the Friends of Literature, a 54 year old Chicago organization devotd to identifyng and honoring the best works in contemporary writing. He established the art gallery at Oakton College. Annual scholarships in his honor are awarded to Oakton students who have demonstrated excellence in the study of art and humanities. Dr. Koehnline is a sculptor whose works have been discussed in a 30 minute television program which aired in Chicago. Active in community affairs, he serves on six local boards."

I say to you that this is really printed on the program's cover.

Of Irwin Shaw I can only say his mastery of the art of fiction, the art of the novel, is shamefully ignored in our time. In particular his chronicles of facing impending death, *Bread Upon The Waters* and *Acceptable Losses,* choke me up. His description of the way Lucy Crown is seen to enjoy sex, towards the end of the novel that bears her name, is one of the most sparkling observations of Woman ever made by a mere mortal male (somewhere in the morass of *From Here to Eternity* by James Jones there is a similar one); and the panorama outlined in *Rich Man, Poor Man* and continued in *Beggarman, Thief* must eventually come to be recognized as one of the great family tales in all literature or there is truly, truly, truly no justice in the world! Now as of November 20, 2008, the article on *Rich Man, Poor Man* from Wikipedia was 99% my work. I don't know if anyone has since cut it to ribbons, as Wiki allows. It is as follows:

Rich Man, Poor Man is a <u>novel</u> written by <u>Irwin Shaw</u> in 1969. It is the last of the novels of Shaw's middle period before he began to concentrate, in his last works such as Evening In Byzantium, Nightwork, Bread Upon The Waters, and Acceptable Losses, on the inevitability of impending death.

The novel is a sprawling work, with 665 pages, and covers many of the themes Shaw returns to again and again in all of his fiction - Americans living as expatriates in Europe, the McCarthy era, children trying to break away from the kind of life lived by their parents, social and political issues of capitalism, the pain of relationships. On the very first page Shaw subtly telegraphs the sad ending of the story, in the same way that the first scene of a film will often quote the last scene.

Originally published as a short story in *Playboy Magazine*, it became an international bestseller when published as a novel. The bulk of the novel concerns the three children of Mary Pease and Axel Jordache - the eldest, Gretchen, the middle child, Rudolph, and the youngest, Thomas. It chronicles their experiences from the end of World War 2 until the late 1960s.

In the early parts of the novel Shaw goes to great lengths to make the point about "Jordache blood" - violent, bitter, resentful. One of the ways he does this is by meticulously describing the hate-filled marriage of the parents, Mary and Axel. The novel is told in the third person omniscient point of view but never wholly objectively, often through the lens of the consciousness of one of the five family members. When told through the POV of either Mary or Axel the view of humanity, and of the Jordache family, is relentlessly bleak and pessimistic.

The tripwire that sets all of the ensuing plot action in motion occurs when Gretchen Jordache begins an affair with the president of the company she works for, Teddy Boylan, a man much older than herself. Eventually her brothers Rudolph and Thomas also become involved with Boylan, in different ways, and it is his influence upon all three that first springs each of them into the world beyond the small upstate New York town where their parents scrape by with their bakery. Boylan constitutes their first true encounters with an adult beyond their parents.

Many people, mainly because of their familiarity with the <u>miniseries</u> rather than the actual source material, thought of the story as a very simplistic juxtaposition of the virtuous, goody two shoes brother (Rudolph) with the black sheep, ne'er-do-well younger sibling (Thomas, whom Shaw seeks to differentiate psychologically by means of a physical symbol - he is the only blond haired member of the family), but the novel is much more complex than this in its demonstrative understructure. For example Rudolph is constantly developing positive relationships only with people who can help him - his father, Mr. Calderwood, Johnny Heath, Boylan. In stark contrast to this both Gretchen and Thomas consistently entangle themselves with the kinds of people that modern self help literature calls "drain people" or "toxic people". A couple of examples: Thomas' only friend in the world, Claude, gives him up immediately to the authorities the second his own well being is threatened, and when Axel Jordache learns of Tom's actions his only impulse is to get rid of him, to send him away to live with family in Ohio. Contrast this with Rudolph's friend, Johnny Heath, who becomes his lifelong friend, attorney, and business partner, and also with what Axel Jordache does when confronted by Rudolph's French teacher over a behavior miscue - he slaps the teacher in the face. We cannot imagine him defending either Gretchen or Thomas in this manner.

Boylan serves as the maguffin that drives the plot for all three of the Jordache siblings. For Gretchen he is an introduction to the world of men and relationships. He awakens in her the realization that she is the kind of woman who reduces men to cowering wimps but who cannot, perhaps somewhat paradoxically, put together a sound, completely fulfilling relationship. Her marriage to Willie Abbott collapses under the weight of his alcoholism and her marriage to Colin Burke ends in tragedy when Burke dies in a car accident. Similarly none of her numerous affairs bear any genuine emotional fruit.

It is because of Boylan that Thomas embarks on a savage act of vandalism (with his friend Claude, who eventually turns him in). When caught, the men of the town present Axel Jordache with a choice - send Thomas away or let him and the family face the consequences with the law. Jordache sends him away to live with his brother in Ohio, thus beginning a pattern that is repeated over and over and over in the novel: Thomas settles somewhere for a while, does OK for a time, then gets into trouble and has to flee.

Finally Boylan offers to pay for Rudolph to go to college. Although on one level Rudolph despises Boylan as a petty vindictive rich pervert of an old man, he sees another side of him as well - the financially independent man of the world who wants for nothing. Shaw uses Rudolph's even, balanced judgment of Boylan as a counterpoint to the wholly negative, wholly one sided opinion of him both Gretchen and Thomas, in their own separate ways, cling to.

It's almost painfully hard for me to comment on the Lew Archer novels of Ross Macdonald, so I won't get into this too much. I merely present an unfinished essay I once had on one of my websites long ago:

Ross Macdonald's The Wycherly Woman (1961)

The first of Ross Macdonald's novels featuring private eye Lew Archer, *The Moving Target,* appeared in 1949; the last, *The Blue Hammer,* in 1976. There are eighteen in all. The uncountable numbers of editions of these books carry quotes such as "The finest series of detective novels ever written by an American" and "The American private eye - immortalized by Hammett, refined by Chandler, brought to its zenith by Macdonald." It's tempting to dismiss quotes like these as hype, but in Macdonald's case the hype is probably true. Beginning with the *The Galton Case* in 1959 Macdonald's work began to ascend to a level of excellence that Hammett and Chandler could only dream of. There, too, critics and reviewers first began to really understand that what Macdonald was writing were Freudian family tragedies disguised as gumshoe yarns. In certain of Macdonald's books, for example *The Chill* or *The Underground Man,* the suspense is so nerve wracking, the endings so surprising, that the uninitiated might be well advised to read with a bottle of ibuprofren handy. The novel we consider here, *The Wycherly Woman,* is not at that level for those categories, but it is for another - the category of sin. Another quote that frequently appears on the covers of the Archer stories is "Most mystery writers write about crime - Ross Macdonald writes about sin." Indeed. Turning the last few pages of *The Wycherly Woman* makes us understand how very real the problem of evil in the world is, has always been, and probably always will be. More - it makes us see how far beyond things like politics and social problems true evil really is. It isn't concerned with things like that, it doesn't come from things like that. It has a wholly metaphysical character. It comes from some kind of abstruse netherworld that is perhaps beyond empirical understanding. On the last page we see that only Lew Archer and the murderer know the truth of the unspeakable actions that lie at the root of the case, and that, even though Archer will turn the killer over to the law with a confession of the murders, he will not tell anyone the real motivation behind them. The whole thing is simply too evil.

Homer Wycherly is a wealthy businessman who hires Archer to look into the disappearance of his daughter Phoebe who vanished two months ago. Archer is immediately plunged into a whirlpool of lies, deceit, confusion, blackmail, double deals, and mistaken identities when he interviews some people at the girl's college dorm. Macdonald's ability to describe people operating under acute psychological stress is so precise it almost seems like it was beamed here from another planet. This is how he describes Phoebe's boyfriend Bobby Doncaster's reply after Archer grills him with a tough question:

"I have no ideas on the subject." But he had ideas. They flickered darkly at the back of his green eyes like fish in waters too deep for identification.

The scholarship on Macdonald is rather voluminous (Professor Marlings's, for example, is very well done http://www.case.edu/artsci/engl/marling/hardboiled/ Macdonald.HTM); I can't pretend to have a lot to add. However, after a short summary of the beginning of the plot we might look at a few things that have not received much attention in a lot of the existing writing on Macdonald's writings.

Archer starts from the day the girl disappeared. Then, Homer Wycherly was on a docked luxury liner, waiting to embark on a cruise. Phoebe was also on board to wish her father bon voyage. In short order who should show up but his ex-wife, the girl's mother, Catherine. She creates quite a scene, screaming, cursing, yelling, making accusations and demands, hitting ship's officers when they try to remove her, etc. It's all about money, and she wants more of it from Homer Wycherly. Eventually Phoebe is revealed to be the only one who can calm her mother down, and the two of them leave the ship together. The old man Wycherly tells Archer it's the last time he saw either one of them alive. The question is left unasked, but it cannot fail to raise itself in reader's minds - why is a woman, so well provided for in divorce from her rich husband, hurting so badly for money? Archer goes to her house to ask her, but upon arrival he finds the place locked up and boarded, with a For Sale in front. Seeking answers, he goes to the office of the real estate broker whose name is on the sign, Ben Merriman, and finds not Merriman but his unhappy wife, who passes the hours in a thick haze of alcohol. Convincing her he's a buyer who may want to make an offer on the house, Archer gets the keys. Inside he discovers a corpse, the face beaten in so badly as to be unrecognizable, but ID on the body shows it to be Ben Merriman the real estate man. Some more clues lead to a man named Stanley Quillan who runs a sound recording studio; tailing Quillan, Archer discovers that he goes - guess where? - to Ben Merriman's real estate office. Eavesdropping at a window, he learns that Quillan and Merriman's wife are brother and sister and, moreover, that Merriman and Quillan had some kind of powerful secret knowledge about the Wycherly woman that they were blackmailing her with. In short order Quillan also turns up dead, shot in the head in his studio, and thus the two questions: What did Merriman and Quillan know about Catherine Wycherly, and why was it so important that somebody would kill them to keep it quiet? The case that ensues is like a roller coaster ride from the depths of hell, as Archer talks to numerous witnesses and suspects who each contribute a tiny piece of the master puzzle.

But they each contribute without knowing it. Lew Archer is the only one who sees things with complete lucidity (although even this is only at the very end), and this is the first point I'd like to raise. Last year the film *Babel* tried to make the point that communication is very hard, that simply to transmit a coherent, understandable thought to another person can sometimes be quite a challenge. In Macdonald's novels this kind of communication breakdown approaches a 100% saturation level. Everybody talks, nobody listens or comprehends. People say things that in reality turn out to mean something opposite, or different, from what the speaker intends. At one juncture a character says, "Your father did this to me," and a third character overhears. The description "your father" denotes a different person to each of the three in the scene, just as "this" in "did this" represents three different states of affairs to the three characters involved. Obviously such a world is going to be chock full of sorrows. To take another example - throughout practically the whole story Archer is trying to find a certain cab driver who was seen picking up Phoebe Wycherly near the cruise ship. He finally does, and he asks him to show him where he took her. It turns out to be a shady hotel. When Archer begins questioning him about whether or not he carried her bags up to the room, the man completely misunderstands and thinks Archer is accusing him of rape or crimes of perversion.

Of course there were other considerations, as well, for selecting the name of this character. Augustine and Travis McGee can rather easily be emulated in dress and mood, but how would one make oneself up to resemble Irwin Shaw? Bellow? Baldwin? Updike? Or any of their characters? (Lew Archer might be comparatively easily recreated, but I ask you if he is unique enough. What would distinguish him from Sam Spade or Philip Marlowe?)

(7) Quoted from *Bright Orange for the Shroud*. I remember once reading the stuffed shirt Martin Seymour-Smith referring to John D. Macdonald as a hack. What an utterly amazing mischaracterization and misunderstanding. (Although in the same book he perceptively and accurately called Hubert Selby Jr. the first and only novelist to write in the stream of consciousness style with complete success.)

(8) It's perhaps deeply instructive to contrast this very low moment in the history of the Coca Cola corporation

with one of its highest moments - the admission that "New Coke" in the 1980s was a disastrous mistake. Comparison of the way Ivester worked with the way earlier Coke executives Roberto Goizueta and Donald Keogh handled the New Coke fiasco is a great lesson in human relations and life skills. Ivester also botched a situation in Belgium over contaminated Coke that was making children sick. I believe it was Warren Buffet, the chief stockholder in Coke at the time, who told Ivester investors had lost confidence in his leadership of the company.

(9) Is it me, or does the Seattle restaurant *How To Cook A Wolf* have a profoundly unappealing website?

(10) The pessimistic Italian poets such as Montale and Leopardi ("Night Song of a Wandering Asian Shepherd") held a huge attraction for me in youth.

(11) This, like Ross Macdonald's Lew Archer novels, is too painful for me to really comment on. William Barrett's book *The Illusion of Technique* contains, in the earlier chapters, a discussion of Wittgenstein's *Tractatus* that is for me the zenith of discourse on religion and religious matters.

(12) It's even unclear to me, Quinones, right now as I write this, what I mean exactly or what I want to have my narrator mean. Several principles from Greene's *The Art of Seduction* seem to apply here, for example 3. Send Mixed Signals; 15. Isolate The Vicitm; or even 2.Create A False Sense of Security - Approach Indirectly. Also, from *The 48 Laws of Power*, 36. Disdain Things You Cannot Have: Ignoring Them Is The Best Revenge seems to have some relevance, as does 4. *Create a Sense of Urgency and Desperation:*

The Death Ground Strategy from *The 33 Strategies of War*. **At this time we might take a moment to see if the way that Peter decides to deal with Myla in the supermarket is or is not a practical application of these two principles - Disdain Things You Cannot Have - Ignoring Them Is The Best Revenge and Create A Sense Of Urgency and Desperation: The Death Ground Strategy.**

For purposes of economy, here, I'll concentrate on the latter. Readers are invited to investigate the former according to their own specific levels of interest and desire.

The character, Peter, wants to play it cool with Myla - with whom, in the final analysis, he knows he really has no chance; he's hoping against hope; therefore, he places himself on "death ground" with her by seeming to be uninterested. The chance he takes, of course, is that the plot will backfire and she'll accept his disinterest at face value and take it literally. In Robert Greene's book The 33 Strategies of War *the idea is paraphrased as follows:*

You are your own worst enemy. You waste precious time dreaming of the future instead of engaging in the present. Since nothing seems urgent to you, you are only half involved in what you do. The only way to change is through action and outside pressure. Put yourself in situations where you have too much at stake to waste time or resources - if you can't afford to lose, you won't. Cut your ties to the past; either enter unknown territory where you must depend on your wits and energy to see you through. Place yourself on "death ground" where you back is against the wall and you must fight like hell to get out alive.

Greene offers subdivisions of the principle, with examples. One such is "The No Return Tactic" with Hernan Cortes burning his ships in Mexico, forcing himself and his men to stay and fight and conquer. He completely removed the options of fleeing and escaping. A second example is "The Death At Your Heels Tactic" which discusses Dostoevsky writing his great novels under extreme pressure, the memory of having once almost been executed by the czar burning in his brain. In his exegesis Greene writes:

Death is impossible for us to fathom; it is so immense, so frightening, that we will do almost anything to avoid thinking about it. Society is organized to make death invisible, to keep it several steps removed. That distance may seem necessary for our comfort, but it comes with a terrible price: the illusion of limitless time, and a consequent lack of seriousness about daily life. We are running away from the one reality that faces us all. As a warrior in life, you must turn this dynamic around: make the thought of death something not to escape but to embrace. Your days are numbered. Will you pass them half awake and halfhearted or will you live with a sense of urgency?

As an aside, for the record I point out that a comtemporary book on Stoicism by William B. Irvine discusses this exact idea in a slightly different context. Irvine calls it "negative visualization."

Returning to Greene: some more subdivisions of the principle: "Stake Everything On A Single Throw" in which LBJ's first run for Congress, in Texas, in 1937, is discussed; "Act Before You Are Ready" discusses Caesar crossing the Rubicon; "Enter New Waters" talks about some bold, previously unheard of types of moves Joan

Crawford made in Hollywood; "Make It 'You Against The World'" tells of Ted Williams' deliberate strategy of picking fights with the baseball press; and finally "Keep Yourself Restless And Unsatisfied" discusses Napoleon.

Mikhail Tal was the eighth official world chess champion and one of the most dazzling attacking players of all time. Tal would play devastating sacrifices that usually led to unstoppable mating attacks, and he skyrocketed to the world championship at a very young age. However, modern computer analysis has shown that many of Tal's bold sacrifices were unsound, and that there were refutations available. It was just that in official match and tournament play, with the clock ticking and much prestige and money on the line, opponents more often than not could not find the right moves under such psychological pressure. Thus Tal placed himself on "death ground" by gambling that his rivals would be unable to unravel his mysteries.

In the 2008 US presidential campaign John McCain was behind Barack Obama in every poll and badly needed a 'game changer', something to shake up the race and tip the scales in his favor. Everyone watched and waited to see who he would choose as his running mate. Comparatively safe, boring choices were continually analyzed in the media - Pawlenty? Romney? Huckabee? When McCain announced that he had selected Alaska Gov. Sarah Palin, the media and the country went into an absolute hysteria. Palin gave a speech at the Republican convention that shook the rafters and turned the dynamics of the race around completely. McCain gained a "bounce" and started to lead in all the polls. Obama was thrown on the defensive. It was the only time in the two year long campaign where he and his team appeared badly confused, clearly caught totally off guard. They issued contradictory statements about Palin within hours; on the stump, Obama made the horrible mistake of talking about Palin as though he were running against her instead of McCain. Of course, through a series of poor decisions and strategic blunders the McCain-Palin candidacy soon fizzled completely, but in the bold, caution-to-the-winds pick of Palin John McCain showed himself perfectly willing to place himself on "death ground."

And so it is an open question as to whether or not our character Peter, in his 'pursuit' of the goddess Myla, made the right decision in adopting the "death ground" strategy. That will not be discussed or resolved here. Perhaps what is most interesting are the questions, Why would he adopt the "death ground" strategy in the first place? Why does he need to? Is he desperate for women in general, or is it specifically for Myla? Does he REALLY want Myla in some important way, or is it all a game? Peter's remarks about his relations with women are vague, and their timeline is wholly unclear (the chronology is unavailable), so we basically have to guess, to make stabs at facts.

Printed in the United States
By Bookmasters